KU-146-962

RIDE FOR THE RIO!

Will Hooper was a sodbuster and Lee Earl was a cowboy. They'd spent their entire lives on different sides of the fence. But then something terrible happened to make each man look beyond his own petty hatreds — like the outrage that occurred one stormy night at Will's farm. So, when the sodbuster crossed the Rio Grande to settle a score with a dirty little Mexican with murder on his mind, the cowboy was right beside him . . .

GLENN LOCKWOOD

RIDE FOR THE RIO!

Complete and Unabridged

LINFORD
Leicester

First published in Great Britain in 2000 by
Robert Hale Limited
London

First Linford Edition
published 2001
by arrangement with
Robert Hale Limited
London

The moral right of the author has been asserted

Copyright © 2000 by David Whitehead
All rights reserved

British Library CIP Data

Lockwood, Glenn, *1958* –
Ride for the Rio!.—Large print ed.—
Linford western library
1. Western stories
2. Large type books
I. Title
823.9'14 [F]

ISBN 0–7089–9736–8

LINCOLNSHIRE
COUNTY COUNCIL

Published by
F. A. Thorpe (Publishing)
Anstey, Leicestershire
Set by Words & Graphics Ltd.
Anstey, Leicestershire
Printed and bound in Great Britain by
T. J. International Ltd., Padstow, Cornwall

This book is printed on acid-free paper

For Janet

1

Rape is a terrible word: an even more terrible deed.

The thought whispered through Rafael Ugarte's mind as he stood in the doorway of the run-down barn, his haunted brown eyes fixed on the house on the far side of the night-blackened yard.

Hiding there in the shadows, where the weak moonlight couldn't touch him, he wrestled with the deep sense of shame that threatened to engulf him. After all, the woman had struck him as a kindly soul. From the moment they had arrived, she had shown them nothing but hospitality. And that made it all the more unthinkable that he could just stand by and allow this outrage to continue now.

He knew what he *should* do, but he hesitated to follow the demands of his conscience because the perpetrator of the outrage, Alesandro Larraya de Benedictus, was his master. And Rafael, born into a family of servants, raised in a land where the rich held sway and the poor obeyed without question and often in fear of their lives, was his majordomo. Obedience had been bred into him. It was instinctive.

But this time . . .

This time it was *different*.

The whores of his native Mexico, they were used to poor treatment, and Alesandro paid them well to suffer it. In his own land, suffering was a way of life. But things here in *Los Estados Unidos* were not as they were south of the border.

As respectfully as he could, he had tried to tell Alesandro as much, but, born to privilege, Alesandro had grown to manhood with complete disregard for the opinions of others. Alesandro listened only to his own dark desires.

In the distance, the parting storm continued to rumble ominously, and occasional forks of lightning flared jaggedly through the heavy sky further south. Made restless by the storm, the horses which had drawn their elegant brougham to this lonely place suddenly stirred and nickered plaintively, and, glad of the momentary distraction, Rafael turned and crossed the hay-strewn floor to reach up and scratch at their big, velvety muzzles and offer a few words of comfort.

He was a big man, broad of shoulder, deep of chest, his tanned face weighed down by a heavy brow, a prominent nose, thick lips and a lantern jaw. His size and weathered ugliness, coupled with the Colt .45 tied at his right hip, gave him an impression of toughness and durability. And certainly he was tough. But if you looked into his eyes, you saw also that he was gentle, God-fearing, sensitive to the wishes of others.

That was why he sheltered there in the darkness of the barn, stroking the horses and trying so hard to pretend

3

that none of this was really happening.

It had all started when Alesandro's father, Don Miguel, had sent them north to buy breeding stock — Herefords, mostly, but Durhams and Brahmans too, if they could find them — to improve the bloodlines of their own vast Iberian herds. It was the first time Don Miguel had entrusted his beloved Alesandro with such an important chore, the first time Alesandro had left his own country and, just like a child let loose in a candy store, he had been determined to sample everything Mexico's rich neighbour had to offer.

Thus, it had fallen to Rafael to handle Don Miguel's business, to haggle for the best prices and arrange for delivery of the merchandise. Alesandro had been too busy with all the distractions the Lone Star State had to offer, principally its rich whiskey and dance-hall floozies.

In all, they had stayed but a week in the dusty cow-town that had grown up around the army outpost of Camp

Lincoln, but to Rafael it had seemed much longer. And so reckless had the boy's behaviour been during that time that, had he not been the son of Don Miguel, he would almost certainly have ended up in jail.

Firstly there had been some trouble with a whore who had not bargained on the suffering she had been forced to endure in the name of Alesandro's warped pleasure. And then there was the shooting which had erupted when Alesandro had been caught cheating at cards. Fortunately, Rafael had been on hand both times to buy the aggrieved parties off with Don Miguel's expense money before they could press charges and bring dishonour to the name of Benedictus.

As it was, the fact that he was Don Miguel's son gave him some measure of immunity. But even so, it was with no small relief — at least as far as Rafael was concerned — that they finally set off on the first leg of their long journey back to Nuevo Oro, 150 miles south, with Alesandro lounging in the brougham and Rafael sitting up on the high seat, the reins twisted around his big, work-hardened fists.

As Camp Lincoln fell behind them and the afternoon waned, however, the sky began to darken and a cool wind sprang up. Rafael, recognizing the signs, turned his eyes to the heavens. A storm was coming, and they would be wise to seek shelter before it arrived. The only trouble was, this southern Texas border country was all sage and buffalo grass, the seemingly endless, rippling prairie through which ran the rutted trail south dotted here and there by clusters of blue and white columbines. There was hardly any shelter to speak of, maybe the odd, faraway stand of cottonwoods, but little more.

One hour and seven miles later, the storm struck.

It struck with all the force for which the storms in these parts were famous. A sudden gust of wind, stronger than the rest, slapped at the coach and

Alesandro let go a stream of curses as Rafael fought desperately to keep the vehicle from overturning. In the next second, forked lightning reached down to discharge itself into the ground barely a quarter of a mile away, and then came a hissing, pounding wall of water that hit the coach with a billion ice-cold needles, and after that — if such were possible — things quickly grew worse.

The flat Texas countryside quickly became a mire. Mud sucked at the coach wheels and more than once Rafael had to climb down and dig them free with his bare hands. All the while, Alesandro cursed both the *gringo* weather and Rafael's stupidity in getting them stuck out here in the first place, not once offering to step down and lend a hand.

Ah, he was spoilt, that one. Spoilt and petulant and selfish . . . but just like his indulgent father, Rafael overlooked his faults. He had been twenty when Alesandro was born. Now Alesandro was twenty-five. He had watched Alesandro grow from baby to boy, from boy to adolescent, from adolescent to man. And in devoting himself to his master's care, he had learned also to love him as a father loves his son.

The storm worsened, and it became increasingly difficult to control the nervous horses. They struggled on for another mile, maybe even less. Then, eyes narrowed against the sting of the rain, his pocked olive skin running with water, Rafael turned his head to call down his intention of heading for a skimpy stand of timber he'd spotted in the distance, but stopped even before the first word could leave his mouth. For in that moment he had spotted something else — the beckoning amber glow of a lamplit window.

'Looks like a ranch away to the east, *jefe*,' he called. 'With luck we shall find shelter there tonight.'

'And food,' Alesandro called back. 'I'm starving!'

Rafael wheeled them into the yard

fifteen minutes later, by which time the tilled, rain-swamped fields and the heady stink of cabbages and manure had told their own story.

'Bah!' complained Alesandro. 'This isn't a ranch, Rafael! You've brought us to a *farm*!' He made the word sound dirty, for he, like cattlemen on both sides of the border, hated farmers with a vengeance. They fenced off the open range, stole good grazing land the cattlemen had traditionally considered their own and ruined it with their ploughs and pitiful rows of wheat, alfalfa and vegetables. In the circumstances, however, he couldn't afford to be fussy, so he said no more.

Rafael, who shared none of his master's prejudices, brought the brougham to a grateful halt before a single-storey clapboard and clay-chinked house with a brick chimney and a sagging porch. A quick glance showed them a barn and very little else, no livestock to speak of, just a windmill squeaking and swaying madly some little distance away and a small, open-sided shed crammed with farming implements.

He climbed down and splashed awkwardly up onto the porch. The lifeless, splintered boards groaned beneath his weight, and as he hammered on the door, rainwater wormed beneath the collar of his waist-length suede jacket and slip-slid down his spine, making him shiver. A moment passed, and then a woman's voice called hesitantly through the flimsy panels, 'Who is it? Who's there?'

'Travellers, *señora*,' Rafael called back in halting but passable English. 'Seeking only permission to shelter in your barn.'

Another moment's hesitation, and then a silhouette appeared briefly at one of the small, rain-streaked, lamp-yellowed windows. He stood back, allowing her to see him, to see that he posed no threat, and then he heard the sound of a bar being lifted on the other side of the door, and the door itself

10

swung partway open with a painful grating of dry hinges.

Light from the lamp set in the centre of the poor-looking room showed him a woman in a white blouse and coarse brown country skirt. She was about thirty, of medium height and good, womanly proportions. She wore her long, auburn hair combed back from a well-structured, sun-reddened face with a straight nose, firm lips and strong chin. But fear still lingered in her very pale-blue eyes, and he moved quickly to dispel it.

'A thousand apologies for the disturbance, *señora*. I am Rafael Ugarte, from the *rancho* of Don Miguel Larraya de Benedictus of Nuevo Oro, Coahuila Province. My master and — '

A creak of boards told him that Alesandro had climbed out of the coach and hurried up onto the porch beside him, and he turned as Alesandro swept off his big sombrero and bowed gallantly at the waist. '*Buenas noches, señora*,' he said with a flash of strong

11

white teeth. 'Please, allow me to introduce myself. I am Alesandro Larraya de Benedictus. We were returning home to Mexico following a business trip to your country when we were caught in this storm. Now we are cold and wet and hungry, and will pay well for food and shelter.'

The woman chewed briefly at her bottom lip Clearly she did not know what to do for the best. Then, doubtless won over by Alesandro's charming manner, she relaxed a shade and told them that she was Mrs Jane Hooper, that she was sorry for being so cautious, it was nothing personal, and to come inside. Rafael held back, said he would first quarter the horses and coach in the barn, but as far as Alesandro was concerned, he had already ceased to exist. It was always that way when a pretty woman was around. The youngster brushed past him and followed the woman inside.

Half an hour later, Rafael splashed back across to the house and knocked respectfully at the door. As the woman let him inside, he smelled rabbit stew and his stomach growled in anticipation, for it had been a long afternoon and he hadn't realized just how hungry he was. Alesandro, he saw, was already sitting at the table, smoking a thin black cigarillo and nursing a cup of coffee, his mood expansive.

'Ah, come join me, *compañero*. Señora Hooper here is preparing a feast fit for a king, or so she tells me.'

The woman turned from the poor sheet-iron stove that occupied part of the facing wall and offered Rafael a small, self-conscious, smile. 'It'll hardly be that,' she corrected apologetically. 'I'm afraid my husband and I live a simple life with few frills. The food is plain, but you'll find it hot and filling.'

'We ask for no more, *señora*,' Rafael replied politely, and took his place at the sawbuck table.

As Mrs Hooper turned back to the stove, he threw a quick, curious glance around the poky little room. The misty

13

lamplight showed him some cheap, functional furniture, a few Currier and Ives prints tacked up to brighten the walls, a slim grandmother clock and a broad stone fireplace, but not much else. These Hoopers, he thought, had done their best to make this place a home, but for all that it was still a poor, lonely spot in which to live.

Five minutes later the woman set a plate of sliced bread and a dish of apple butter on the table, then ladled rich, steaming stew into two Burl poplar wood bowls. 'Your husband?' Rafael enquired politely. 'He will not be joining us?'

Before the woman could reply, Alesandro said, 'Señora Hooper's husband went to Sheridan for supplies.'

Something in the way Alesandro said it made Rafael's guts twist up, and all at once he knew what was going through the other man's mind, that here was a young and handsome woman, all alone in the middle of nowhere. That was just how Alesandro *would* think.

Hurriedly, he changed the subject. 'Sheridan? That is quite a distance, is it not, *señora*? Would it not have been easier to go into Camp Lincoln?'

'Yes,' she replied tiredly. 'It would.' But beyond that she would say no more, and he sensed it would not be wise to pursue the matter.

They ate and the food was good. Alesandro was charming and witty, and regaled the woman with stories of life on the Benedictus ranch, a vast, long-established and much-respected enterprise which encompassed more than 200,000 acres of good graze, timber and water far to the south. Mrs Hooper listened politely and allowed that it put their own 160 acres to shame.

At length, Rafael cleared his throat and reminded his master politely that they still had quite a journey ahead of them, but because the storm was still lashing the land outside, Mrs Hooper said they were welcome to bunk down in the barn and be on their way the following morning. Rafael felt his heart sink at that, for it would have been better for them all had he gotten Alesandro away from there as soon as possible.

With thanks, they took their leave and hurried across to the barn. At least, Rafael hurried. Oblivious to the storm now, Alesandro merely swaggered, and the swagger made Rafael feel the bite of the wind more keenly, for he had seen it before and he knew what it meant. They entered the dark barn, where rain drummed insistently against the pitched roof and dripped through gaps in the shingles in long, silvery lines. Searching for the closed lantern he had seen suspended from a peg earlier, Rafael said, 'I will fork some fresh hay into the stalls, *jefe*, make them as dry and warm as I can.'

He found a match and struck it to life just as Alesandro said, 'Make up whatever you like for yourself, *compañero*. Me, I think I will be spending this night on a feather mattress.'

16

Rafael froze, then deflated just a little. Well, he thought. There it was. Confirmation of his worst fear. Carefully he lit the lamp, blew out the match and turned to face his young charge. Alesandro was still standing in the barn doorway, a tall, slender man whose expensively tailored brown suede charro jacket and matching flared pants accentuated his height and build.

Rafael looked into his face. Alesandro was handsome, his smooth skin the colour of milky coffee. But there was cruelty there, also. He could not deny it. There, in the set of the full, almost womanly lips, the flare of the small, delicate nostrils, the depths of the near-black eyes.

He said, 'For pity's sake, *jefe* — '

Alesandro glanced at him, a half-smile playing across his mouth. 'Spare me your entreaties, Rafael. Did you really think a Benedictus would ever bed down in a barn? And while such a pretty one was available?'

'But she is not available, *jefe*. She is

married to another — '

' — who is not here to object.'

Rafael shook his head. 'In the name of the Almighty, *jefe*! The woman has shown us nothing but kindness. Is this how you repay her? By going over there and forcing yourself upon h — '

Alesandro moved in a blur, his right hand streaking up and across to slap his servant into silence. For that one instant the latent cruelty came boiling to the surface, and it was an ugly, ugly thing to see.

Rafael rocked back on his heels, and though spirit flashed briefly in his eyes, he made no move to retaliate. That would have been unthinkable. Thunder growled above them, making the loose boards shake and buzz momentarily. Then Alesandro said in a soft, danger-ous voice, 'You will never take that tone with me again, Rafael. *Comprende usted?*'

Rafael's eyes dropped from Alesan-dro's face, and though he dwarfed the other man, Alesandro was the giant there right then.

'*Comprende?*' Alesandro said again.

'*Si, señor,*' Rafael whispered meekly. '*Perdon.* I . . . I forgot myself. But your father would never forgive me if I did not at least caution you. This woman, she is a *good* woman, and kind. You heard her. She and her man live a hard life out here. I beg you, do not make it any harder for them.'

Alesandro only grinned. 'One night with me and she will forget her hard life.'

'I'm *begging* you, Alesandro! This woman, she's not just another whore who can be bought off. She is a *gringo* woman . . . and I know these Texas men. They do not stand to see them abused.'

Alesandro dismissed him with an irritable wave of the hand. 'Ah, you worry too much. And you don't know women as well as you think you do. This one, she will thank me for brightening her miserable life before I am through with her.'

'Alesandro — '

But Alesandro only laughed and swaggered back across the yard, rain darkening the shoulders of his expensive waist-length jacket and bouncing off the brim of his black sombrero, and Rafael watched him go, shaking his head and willing the younger man to have a change of heart and come back to the barn.

But Alesandro did not have a change of heart. And that was a tragedy. For Rafael knew that no good would come of this night's actions. No good at all . . .

* * *

He stood watching the house for a long time after Señora Hooper opened the door and allowed Alesandro to go back inside. He tried to tell himself that Alesandro had been right, that he did know women better than a stupid old bachelor like Rafael. But deep down, he knew it was not so. To have his way with this woman, Alesandro was going to have to force himself upon her, and he would, too. Little words like *no*, or *please*, or *don't*, had never stopped him in the past . . .

Just then he heard a sound across the yard and a feeling of dread seized him. There, *again*! A thud, as of someone slamming against a wall, and then a cry of pain that was quickly stifled by a tirade of angry Spanish.

Mouth dry, wanting desperately to shut out the sounds of what was happening, Rafael walked in a tight, helpless circle, his mouth working in a feverish prayer. *Please, dear Lord, please don't let this be happening.* Another thud, another scream. *I beg you. Lord, please make it stop, make it stop!*

It stopped.

Rafael stumbled back to the doorway and leaned against the frame. He felt sick at himself for standing by and doing nothing and his head ached so much that he thought it might burst. In that moment, he hated both himself and Alesandro — but he hated himself more.

He had heard how Alesandro abused his women, of course, cursing them and beating them all in the name of pleasure. Dear God, he was sick in the head, and he, Rafael, should have done more to curb his vile perversions when he was younger. But what could he do? He was just a servant.

So it was that he stood in the barn doorway and did nothing.

His lips continued to move as he prayed silently for the woman, for his master, for himself. An eternity later he heard a door open on the other side of the yard, and Alesandro stepped down off the porch. He was bareheaded, his hat held loosely in one hand, his fine, embroidered white shirt unbuttoned, his thick, oily black hair awry. His arms hung lifelessly at his sides, his steps, as he splashed through the sucking, muddy puddles, slow and weak.

Having spent his lust, he had become

just a boy again, a tired and peculiarly unhappy boy.

Rafael watched him walk into the light of the turned-low lantern. He saw by the scratches on Alesandro's smooth, tanned face that the woman had fought him right to the end, saw also by the fire that still lingered in his master's eyes that Alesandro had eventually beaten her into obedience.

When Alesandro finally halted and looked at him, there was no longer anything handsome or charming about him. His glazed eyes were red-rimmed and tired, his mouth a frightened line. He made to speak, found that he had screamed himself hoarse at the woman and had to clear his throat before he could try again. 'Make ready for travel,' he husked. 'Let us get away from this place.'

Rafael nodded miserably.

'And, Rafael . . . ?'

'*Si, jefe?*'

Alesandro came closer, reached down and drew Rafael's .45 from its pocket. He looked at the weapon for a while, then turned it around and, holding it by the short barrel, offered it to him, butt-forward.

Rafael said, not comprehending, '*Jefe* . . . ?'

His lower lip trembling now, Alesandro said in his yelled-hoarse voice, 'We cannot leave her alive, *compañero*.'

Rafael's face went slack. 'But — '

'She knows who I am!' the younger man rasped, his eyes big in his face.

'But *jefe*, I cannot — '

Alesandro tightened the fingers of his free hand around Rafael's big right arm. '*Do* it, Rafael!' he hissed. 'You *must*! As long as she lives, she is a threat to me.'

'But — '

'Do it, and . . . and I swear to you, she will be the last. No more. I promise you.'

Rafael looked into his master's face and saw that he was crying.

As he took the proffered gun, he thought dazedly, *Madre de Dios, I have done many things to be ashamed of over the years, but never have I k* — His mind rebelled at the very word, but he forced himself to use it anyway — never before had he killed a woman.

But it was as Alesandro had said. He had given the woman his name. If she made enough of a fuss, she could bring a smear to the name of Benedictus. And in spite of its poverty, Mexico was still a country where honour was everything.

'Can we not . . . buy her silence?' he asked wretchedly. 'I have some of your father's expense money left. Not much, it is true, but enough — '

'This one won't be bought off, Rafael,' Alesandro cut in with grim certainty, sleeving at the scratches on one cheek and leaving a series of red smears in their stead. 'She has pride. Even now.' He shook his head and said, 'No. We have to ensure her silence. And this is the only way.'

Feeling the weight of the weapon dragging at his arm, Rafael thought, Oh, God . . . And sensing his reluctance, Alesandro whispered persuasively, 'Do

25

this thing for me . . . old friend. And then we shall leave this place and never speak of it again.'

He clapped Rafael on the arm, but the gesture was not meant to console him or offer him strength for the task ahead, it was merely meant to get him started back over to the house.

Rafael stumbled across the yard with the gun hanging by his side, and now he too was crying softly. He felt confused, unsure, as if this business were more dream than reality. *Don't do it*, he told himself urgently. *Don't do it, Rafael*. But how could he *not* do it? He *had* to. It was as Alesandro had said. There was no choice.

He thought about the promise his master had made so rashly and shook his head. Not for one moment did he expect Alesandro to keep it. The sickness was so deeply ingrained in him that he would never be able to resist it for long.

Across the yard, up onto the porch, into the darkened house, and all the while, the storm still rumbling behind him.

Into the house . . .

Alesandro watched from the shadows of the barn, his eyes still big and fearful, his slender frame shivering. Had the lust been upon him he knew he would have done the job himself, would have taken his time before pulling trigger in order to prolong his pleasure in the supreme deed. But the lust had deserted him temporarily: he was just a scared little boy now, a scared little boy who wanted Rafael to make everything safe again.

At last the sounds of the storm faded to nothing. The farm sat in quiet, wet silence. Alesandro continued to watch the house, his breath coming very loud from his tight throat, wondering what was taking Rafael so long and cursing him for the delay.

And then it came.

One single, deafening gunblast.

And perhaps a minute or two after that, Rafael staggered back over to the barn, bent double in the doorway and threw up his supper, the supper the woman had so kindly prepared for them.

Neither he nor Alesandro said a word. Neither man dared to even look at the other.

In silence, Rafael set about readying the brougham for travel.

2

At first light the following morning, Will Hooper loaded his supplies aboard his ancient, slat-sided box wagon, harnessed his team-horses and headed for home.

It was a long haul to Sheridan and back, a round trip of better than 150 miles, and he didn't make it any more than he had to because it took him away from the farm for two full days at least, even more if, like the previous day, the weather turned bad and what passed for a trail became impassable. But he'd given up trying to buy his supplies at Camp Lincoln, even though the army town was practically on his doorstep. He wasn't welcome there: Ned Baylock had seen to that.

Still, there was no sense to brooding on it. So, as he kept his heavy-set horses plodding south-east, he cut his green gaze from one side of the worn ribbon of trail to the other, taking pleasure in what he saw there.

The wide open spaces, a great ocean of sun-browned bunchgrass and mesquite and fuzzy stands of oak or elm, pecan or Osage orange, never failed to chase away the blues. He loved the outdoor life, always had. But most of all he enjoyed the isolation of this border country. Out here he could forget all about the ugliness in the world, and imagine that no one else existed save him and Jane.

Thinking of Jane brought the faintest smile to his wide mouth, and not for the first time he told himself he was lucky to have her. She had sand, and sand to spare — and she needed it too, to survive out here. Lord knew, it wasn't an easy life, fighting both the land and the attitudes of their neighbours, but Jane had always told him that as long as he was beside her, she could put up with anything.

Will was a tall man of thirty

summers, with lean flanks and, beneath his collarless shirt and bib overalls, muscular arms and a broad chest. Three years behind a plough, gouging furrows into hard, stubborn Texas soil had done that for him, just as long days beneath the brassy sun had burned his long, rugged face the colour of old copper. As the morning wore on and he drew closer to home, however, more immediate concerns filled his head. In Sheridan he'd picked up rumours that the price of barley was going to come back this year, and he was thinking that maybe he'd put some down and see what happened. He was still thinking about barley when the farm appeared on the distant horizon around the middle of the afternoon, and brought with it another brief smile of anticipation.

Not that he was fooling himself. He knew it wasn't much of a spread. But it was *his*. And there'd been plenty of times — at places like Murfreesboro, Chickamauga and Gettysburg — when even to own this much had seemed like an impossible dream.

But as he tooled the wagon closer to the farm, it suddenly occurred to him that the place looked somehow . . . abandoned.

For a start, there was no sign of Jane anywhere. That in itself was odd. And that wasn't all. By now the chickens should've been let out of the hen house, should've been strutting and clucking and searching for their daily scattering of corn. But the chickens were nowhere to be seen. And Sally, their dairy cow . . . As he drew nearer, he heard her plaintive bawl coming from the shed out behind the cabin, and knew she was complaining because no one had come to milk her yet.

Without warning, the churning in Will's guts suddenly grew more urgent, and he worked the reins quickly to get more speed from his horses. The wagon followed a poor track between wide fields of brown corduroy, each furrow stippled with the first green shoots of this year's wheatyield, and fifteen minutes later he rattled into the yard and brought the wagon to a creaking, harness-tinkling stop in front of the house.

He stood up in the box, his green eyes narrowing on the silent cabin as he waited for Jane to come hurrying outside and set his mind at rest.

He called, hesitantly, 'Jane?'

There was no answer.

Quickly he turned the reins around the brake lever, jumped down, shoved open the cabin door and went inside.

The room was in complete disarray. Everything that could be broken, had been. Chairs had been tipped over, the grandmother clock lay on its side and the table had been shunted across to the far wall. Pictures hung crookedly, and a puddle that stank of stale coffee had gathered in the centre of the floor. The floor itself was littered with shards of broken china, even a couple of pots and pans and a shattered lantern resting in a pool of kerosene.

He shook his head, trying to make

sense out of it all, swept off his broad-brimmed hat to reveal longish, curly hair that was the colour of gold except where the sun had bleached it to a whiter shade of yellow. 'Jane?'

Pure, blind instinct took over then. Throwing the hat aside, he crossed the room in a hurry, his heavy brogans crunching shards of china underfoot and kicking fallen chairs out of his way until he reached the bedroom door. There he closed trembling fingers around the knob, twisted and shoved it wide —

He came up sharp, and his face screwed into a sudden, painful wince.

' . . . Jane?'

She was stretched out on the rumpled bed, and she'd been sleeping, or trying to. But the minute he burst into the room she twitched awake and her head snapped around and he saw that her pale-blue eyes, hardly visible behind swollen, bruise-blackened lids, were glazed with sheer, animal terror.

Confused, baffled, he whispered, 'Jane?'

It *was* Jane, wasn't it? Jesus, the woman on the bed had been beaten so badly it was hard to tell. Her face was puffed up, her lips were split and swollen, her cheeks grazed and bruised. She could've been anyone.

But there was no mistaking the long, auburn hair that fanned out across the pillowslip, or the remnants of the torn white blouse she held around her in a pitiful attempt to retain her modesty.

He thought, *Oh God*. And then he went towards her in a rush, said without even being aware of it, 'Jane, what's happened? What — '

She shook her head, made a desperate mewling sound and pushed up into a sitting position even though the effort brought fresh tears to her fat, painful eyes, and all at once he froze, realizing that she was either so shocked or terrified or both that she didn't even know who he was.

He fought the urge to go to her and

hold her and try to find out just what in hell had been happening here while he'd been in Sheridan, said instead, shakily, 'Jane? Jane, it's me, Will. It's all right now, honey, everything's all right now . . . '

He advanced more cautiously, willing her to recognize him, but she didn't, not at first. She tried to push herself back even further, through the head-board, through the wall if she could manage it, anywhere, just so long as it was away from —

And then he saw something sharpen in those bloodshot eyes, and her cut lips moved soundlessly at first, until a croak of sound that never in a million years could have resembled Jane's voice, said, 'W-Will . . . ?'

He went to her, lowered himself to the edge of the mattress and folded her in his arms, easing his grip a little when she groaned at the pain in her sore ribs and shoulders, and a long time later, when her tears finally ran dry, he fetched a bowl of warm water and tincture of iodine and did what he could to clean her up.

As he worked, she told him all about the two Mexicans, the one who called himself de Benedictus and the other one, the polite one, whose name was Ugarte. But most of all she talked about de Benedictus, and all the things he had done to her.

That brought fresh tears, and a fierce burn of outrage to Will, who quickly set his cloth aside and held her as gently as he knew how, rocked her and told her it was all right now, it was all over.

But Jane wasn't finished yet. Haltingly, as if she could hardly believe it herself, she told him that de Benedictus had intended that she should die here, that she would have but for the compassion of the other man, this giant called Ugarte. Dazedly she told him how Ugarte had come into the darkened house when de Benedictus was done with her, how he had come with a pistol in his fist and tears glistening on his pocked cheeks and found her half-conscious in a corner. He'd bent and picked her up, carried her into the bedroom and set her down on the bed, and then tried as best he could to make her understand that his master was ill and not responsible for his actions. And finally, gesturing with his free hand for her to keep quiet, he'd taken his pistol and fired one single bullet into the opposite wall, then turned and walked out.

She had listened as he and de Benedictus rode out in their fancy wagon. And she remembered that they'd been on their way to a place called Nuevo Oro, in the Mexican province of Coahuila, before the storm had brought them to her door.

Will sagged and told himself he should be grateful to the bigger man, but looking at Jane now, seeing the state she was in, he felt only hatred for both Mexicans.

At last she surrendered to exhaustion and slept, though it was a troubled, fitful, shallow sleep. He stood back and inspected her more closely. Her nose was broken, she had some broken ribs and possibly a broken wrist. Right now she needed more help than he could give her. She needed a doctor. And the only doctor in these parts was the army surgeon at Camp Lincoln.

He went back outside, dragged the supplies out of the wagon and left them where they fell, then went back into the cabin and found some blankets, empty feed-sacks and a coverlet and did what he could to pad the wagon-bed. Finally he went and gathered Jane in his arms and carried her out into the blazing sunshine and lifted her carefully into the wagon.

Still in a state of shock himself, he climbed the big front wheel and sank gratefully onto the spring seat. In the shed behind the cabin, Sally was still complaining, but she would just have to wait. He uncoiled the reins, kicked off the brake and slowly turned the wagon around, working instinctively, his mind still numbed by what had happened.

After all this, he thought. After all we've been through . . .

They'd come out here three years earlier, hoping to make a better life for themselves, and they'd known it wouldn't be easy, because Will was a farmer and he was staking claim to 160 acres right smack in the middle of cattle country. Still, a man had to set his roots down somewhere, and here was as good a place as any.

Not that it mattered to Ned Baylock that he had the law on his side, that he was just taking advantage of the Homestead Act. Baylock, the biggest cattleman in the county, didn't give a cuss that he was only trying to do what any half-decent man wanted to do, to support his wife and build something for the kids he hoped to have one day.

Will could see his point, could even hear Baylock's gravelly voice making it. *You let one goddam sodbuster in an' pretty soon there'll come another, an' another, an' one more after him. Afore you know it, the whole damn' range'll be swarmin' with 'em.*

More than anything else, Baylock wanted to make sure that never happened. So, because the terms of the Homestead Act specified that a man could only gain ownership of his section provided he could manage it and occupy it — for five years, he set out to make Will's life as difficult as he could, to make sure he never lasted the course.

Even then, Will bore the man no malice. He was not a vengeful man by nature. He'd seen his fill of hatred during the late War, and he wanted no more of it. But Baylock had shoved some more of it down his throat, whether he'd wanted it or not. At first he'd come over and tried to buy them out, and when that didn't work he'd started making threats. And making *good* on those threats.

But in taking Will's peaceable nature as a sign of weakness, Baylock had under-estimated his opponent. Against all the odds, Will had held out against him and all the other cattlemen like him for three long years, had always said they'd never squeeze him out, and he'd meant it.

Now, though . . .

Now . . .

* * *

The town which had grown up outside Camp Lincoln was an untidy cluster of clapboard and sod-built structures of varying sizes and heights, the broad main drag, known as Front Street, bordered by two rows of false-fronted stores, saloons and covered boardwalks.

When it came into sight sometime around late afternoon, Will settled himself more firmly on the seat and angled the wagon across the last great swathe of brush country and onto the busy main thoroughfare, ignoring the towners who, having glanced his way and recognized him, hauled up to stare and speculate on what had brought him here.

It was only when the town fell away to the rear and Camp Lincoln itself loomed ahead that he realized how tense he'd become, and he forced himself to release a long-held breath and focus on the imposing sprawl of low adobe buildings with flat, sod roofs and small windows that stretched before him. A flag clung limply to a tall pole at the approximate centre of the outpost, and here and there blue-clad men went about various tasks, fetching, carrying, chopping or sawing firewood, carrying out minor construction work, stable-duty or post clean-up. On the far side of the tree-lined compound, a sergeant was yelling orders at thirty or more recruits, who were marching and wheeling haphazardly with Springfield .45/.70s tilted to their shoulders. No one seemed to pay him much attention.

Because he'd been there a time or two in the past, Will knew the layout of the place and quickly pointed the horses towards the administration block where, after hearing a brief retelling of the facts, a tall, athletic-looking officer who introduced himself as Captain Tom Peckover, sent for the army surgeon. As soon as he arrived, the surgeon, a stick-lean man somewhere in his middle fifties, climbed up into the wagon and bent to examine Jane.

At length he hopped back down into the slanting sunshine and soberly confirmed all the injuries Will had already noted and a few more besides. Then he called for a couple of white-coated orderlies and told them to get Jane out of the wagon and into the infirmary.

Will stood back to give them room, his eyes shuttling anxiously between the orderlies and Jane's pinched, beaten face. Incredibly she was still sleeping, but sleeping so deeply now that he feared she might have lapsed into unconsciousness. 'She'll be all right, won't she?' he asked. 'I mean, she looks so pale . . . '

'She's in shock,' the doctor replied, stroking his sidewhiskers. 'But she's young, strong. No reason why she shouldn't heal, given time — though only time'll tell just what all this's really done to her up here.'

He tapped his forehead.

Will swallowed hard, turned the hat he'd taken off in the doctor's presence nervously in his hands.

As the surgeon strode off after his patient, Peckover asked, 'Have you reported this business to the civilian authorities yet, Mr Hooper?'

Will stared at him blankly. He'd been too preoccupied with Jane to think much about anything else. 'I came straight here.'

'Well, if you'll take my advice, you'll go on back to town and swear out a complaint right away. There's nothing more you can do around here, leastways not until we've done our bit for your wife, and the sooner you alert the law to the matter, the better their chances of catching the men responsible.'

Will nodded. Peckover was right. He needed to swear out a complaint against de Benedictus as soon as possible. Throwing his hat back on, he said, 'I . . . I'll do that, Captain. Thank you.'

To his surprise, the officer extended his right hand and said sincerely, 'I wish you luck, Mr Hooper.'

In a town where the people had been ordered to hate him, he had a feeling he was going to need it.

* * *

The county sheriff's office was a big, blocky building with stockade walls and small windows that was situated midway along Front Street, right next to the public corral. Will braked the wagon out front twenty minutes later, turned his reins around the lever and let himself into a big, cool, clean room with whitewashed walls and a scarred plank floor.

A burly man dressed in a white shirt and brown pants was seated at a roll-top desk set against the facing wall, his back to the door as he pored over a stack of paperwork. Behind a wall of thick iron bars to his right lay a large communal cell, presently unoccupied: to his left stood a polished coal-oil stove. The wall directly above his desk was littered with Wanted posters.

As Will closed the door behind him, the burly man swung around in his padded swivel chair, and the small, etched silver shield of the county sheriff shone briefly against the black leather of his unbuttoned vest.

Frank Doyle was a big-built man somewhere in his forties, with black hair plastered flat to his skull and a thick, wiry beard of the same funereal hue. The beard masked the lower half of a lined, tanned face with dark, tired eyes and a sour, weathered mouth. He gave a slow nod, not seeming especially surprised to find Will standing on the other side of the room, and said, in the careful, measured way he had, 'Hooper. Heard you'd come to town.'

Will took off his hat. 'Came to swear

out a complaint, Sheriff,' he replied.

'Oh?'

'A man came to my place last night . . . he raped my wife and beat her half to death.'

For one brief moment then, it didn't matter that Will was just a sodbuster, or that Jane was just a sodbuster's wife. Surprise, concern and finally anger showed clearly in Doyle's dark eyes. He said slowly, 'She all right?'

Will came a little deeper into the room, again turning his hat by the brim. 'I took her to the surgeon at Camp Lincoln. He's working on her right now.'

'Will she *live*?'

Not trusting himself to speak, Will only nodded.

Doyle fell silent, and Will sensed that he was being torn between a natural impulse to do what he could to bring the rapist to book, and obeying the dictates of Ned Baylock, who'd helped to put him in office and who now more than ever wanted to make Will's life as

48

difficult as he could. At length he said, 'Your woman give you a description of the feller that did it?'

Will nodded. 'She got his name, too. Alesandro Larraya de — ' Even before he finished saying it, he saw recognition cross Doyle's big, ruddy face, and something electric tore through him. 'You *know* him?' he asked urgently.

'There's not a cattleman in these parts who doesn't know his *pa*,' Doyle replied uneasily, emphasising the word *cattleman*. 'You sure you got your facts straight, Hooper? You're making a mighty serious charge, and folks in these parts don't mess with Don Miguel if they can help it.'

'The facts're straight enough, Sheriff. He was travelling with a bigger man named Ugarte. If it hadn't been for him, my wife'd be dead now for sure.'

'And where were you while all this was happening?'

Will knew the lawman was trying to distract him from the main issue, but he answered anyway, and with no small bitterness. 'I was stuck in Sheridan, buying supplies.'

'Well, I'm sorry for your woman,' said the sheriff. 'It's a hell of a thing to've happened, and I hope she gets over it. But there's not a whole lot I can do for you.'

'*What*?'

'I got no jurisdiction beyond the county line, much less across the border,' Doyle replied stiffly.

'But this only happened last night. If we're lucky, he might still be this side of the county line.'

'I doubt it.' Doyle shook his head. 'I'm sorry, Hooper, but I don't see that there's any way I could touch him, even if I knew for sure he was guilty.'

'He *is* guilty.'

'That'd be for the courts to decide.'

'Then ask a judge to sign an extradition warrant. Let's get him back here to stand trial.'

Doyle grunted. 'You'd be wasting your time. Don Miguel'd fight it every step of the way. It could take years to get Alesandro back onto American soil, and even then you got no hard evidence to back you up. It'd be your word against his — and you'd stand no chance against the kind of lawyers Don Miguel could afford.'

'But he raped my *wife*,' Will whispered. 'He damn'-near *killed* her! You telling me there's nothing I can do to make him pay for that, Sheriff?'

'I know it's hard,' Doyle said firmly, 'but that's exactly what I'm telling you.'

Will shook his head, having trouble accepting it. How could the Mexican do what he had and get away with it? It just wasn't —

But then something inside him went cold as understanding finally dawned. He looked at the sheriff for so long that Doyle actually began to squirm a little. 'You say this Don Miguel's well known in these parts?' he asked quietly.

'Well known,' Doyle confirmed, adding pointedly, 'and well respected.'

'I guess that means he does business

with cowmen like Baylock and the rest, then?'

Doyle didn't reply this time. He didn't have to. Will shook his head some more and breathed, 'By God, this doesn't have anything to do with the law, does it? It doesn't even have anything to do with me and Jane being what you people'd call outsiders. It's all about cattlemen sticking together, protecting their investments, even when one of them rough-handles a woman! That's why you won't touch the son, isn't it? Bad for business!'

'I'll forget you said that.'

'*Would* you arrest him, then, if he set foot on American soil again?' Will prodded. 'With his father so all-fired important to Baylock and the others?'

Beneath the beard, Doyle's sour mouth stretched thin. 'Don't push me on this, sodbuster. I've told you the way it is, and I don't like it any more than you do, but that's an end to it.'

Will shook his head, burning now with uncharacteristic fury. 'If you think

I'm gonna let that sonofabitch get away with what he did to my wife, you better think again, Doyle.'

'Now see here — '

'No,' Will cut in, speaking through clenched teeth now, as the heat inside him suddenly turned to something steel-hard, '*you* see *here*. For three years I've taken everything you people've thrown at me. But I'm not gonna take any more. Whether you like it or not, I'm gonna do whatever it takes to bring de Benedictus to trial for what he did to my wife, and neither you, nor Baylock, nor Don Miguel's gonna stop me.'

'I'm warning you, Will Hooper. You'd better not be thinking of taking the law into your own hands — '

Will curled his lip. 'If we had a lawman around here worth his salt,' he said, 'I wouldn't need to.'

Silence, broken only by Frank Doyle's quick, angry breathing, blanketed the room, and for one long, charged moment the sheriff glared at

Will. But here before him stood a new Will, a Will who would sooner die than back down from him. If Doyle hadn't seen the transformation for himself, he likely never would have believed it.

Another moment passed, and then Doyle calmed down, his brawny shoulders sloped, and he said softly, 'Get out of here, Hooper. And don't do anything foolish. You've already got enough enemies in these parts. Mess with Don Miguel and he'll feed your tripes to his dogs.'

3

Will slammed the door behind him and paused a moment on the boardwalk outside. He hadn't felt this angry in years. But he'd meant what he'd told Doyle. De Benedictus was going to pay for what he'd done, and if the law wouldn't do the job for him, he'd damn'-well do it himself.

All at once he wanted to quit this town as quick as he could. After all, there was still a lot to do. If he intended to travel south and catch up with de Benedictus, he'd need a fast horse, supplies, a gun — and to buy those he'd need money, something he'd never had much of.

Then his angry eyes sharpened on the wagon. If he could turn that and the team into hard cash . . .

Squaring his shoulders, he went through the public corral and into the little office at the back of the barn, where the hostler, Artie Bickers, offered to buy the rig and team for forty dollars, take it or leave it. Will had neither the time nor the inclination to dicker, but he was damned if he'd let himself get robbed blind, and Bickers saw as much in his expression. After five minutes' horse-trading, the hostler finally raised his offer to sixty-five dollars, less forty-five for a good saddle horse and a used McClellan saddle.

With money in his pockets now, almost more money than he'd seen at any one time in more than two years, Will started making a mental list of the things he'd need for the forthcoming manhunt. If he rode south by way of the farm, he could help himself to supplies from the wares he'd just fetched back from Sheridan. That only left grain for his newly purchased horse — and a gun.

He hadn't touched a weapon since Appomattox. There'd been no need. If things went the way he hoped they would, there wouldn't be need for one now, except to force de Benedictus to do as he said. His thinking was to get the Mexican back onto American soil, then drag him up to Sheridan, press charges — and make the sonofabitch pay for what he'd done.

It was already well past five in the afternoon, and though the stores stayed open till seven or even eight, most trading was finished for the day. When Will entered Mueller's General Store, Mueller himself was already taking advantage of the quiet time to get started on his inventory. He looked up from his ledgers when Will closed the half-glass door gently behind him and the rheumy eyes behind his small, round spectacles widened briefly in surprise.

'Oh, ah . . . it's, ah, it's Hooper, isn't it? The, ah, farmer?'

Will crossed directly to the counter in the corner, where a selection of weapons were displayed inside a long glass case.

Old man Mueller, watching him nervously, tucked his pen behind one ear and asked, 'You, ah, lookin' for anythin' special, Mr Hooper?'

Will nodded. 'I'll take that Peacemaker.'

Mueller came over but paused before unlocking the case. 'That particular weapon carries a pricetag of, ah, seventeen dollars,' he said discreetly.

As if he hadn't heard him, Will said, 'I'll take a couple boxes of shells, too.'

The storekeeper hesitated a moment longer: then, seeing the look on Will's face, knowing he dare not refuse to serve him, he unlocked the case, reached inside and lifted out a sturdy handgun with a long, grey-steel barrel and hard wearing walnut grips. He handed the weapon over, butt-forward, and Will swallowed softly as he felt its weight and balance.

'You'll, ah, be wantin' a belt for that too, I suppose?'

Will shook his head and handed over some bills, and while Mueller made change, he eased back the hammer, flipped open the loading gate and began to fill five of the six chambers with brasscased bullets. When the gun was filled, he set the hammer down on the empty chamber and tucked it into his deep side pocket.

'Goin' huntin'?' the storekeeper asked uneasily.

Will only glanced at him. 'Good-day, Mr Mueller.'

Entering the barn behind the public corral a few minutes later, he headed directly for the end stall, where he'd been told he could pick up his horse, a thin-legged chestnut roan, when he was ready to ride. He was halfway along the dusty aisle when the silhouettes of four men appeared in the big doorway at the far end of the place and fanned out in a silent line, facing him.

Immediately Will slowed to a stop, for though he didn't recognize three of the newcomers, there was no mistaking the big, broad-shouldered figure of the fourth, who was leaning heavily on a thick, gnarled cane.

Ned Baylock said in that gravelly way of his, 'Been waitin' on you, Hooper.'

Ignoring him for a moment, Will concentrated on his three companions. Though he still didn't know any of them, he knew their type. Their big-brimmed hats and collarless cotton shirts, heavy denim workpants and stove-pipe boots hung with nickel work-spurs identified them as cowboys. But these men were tougher than the usual run of cowboy. The guns sitting high on their hips told him that, and so did the cold insolence in their eyes. These, he knew, were Baylock's elite, the men he kept on his payroll for *special* duties.

'Hear you've had some trouble,' rasped Baylock.

At last Will's eyes sharpened on the rancher.

Everything about Ned Baylock was big. He was nudging sixty now, but the years hadn't withered him any more than the elements had. He was still six feet three inches of pure, mean cussedness. He still tipped the scales at 200 pounds, the same fighting weight he'd been practically all his life. And that face — long, pared down by a hard, outdoor life to little more than skin stretched across a skull that was all cheekbones and granite jaw.

Beneath his big Plainsman hat, Baylock was also as bald as an egg. His face was hairless, too. He didn't even have eyebrows. Just a small, well-clipped moustache the same colour as rust, and two small spots of colour high on those pronounced, surprisingly pale cheeks. The sunken, flesh-creased eyes were blue and ruthless, the mouth no more than a lipless gash.

'They say you're fixin' to take the law into your own hands,' said Baylock.

Will walked closer, slowly, cautiously, until he reached the stall where his worn McClellan saddle had been thrown across the top rail.

Baylock said, 'Cat got your tongue?'

Will glanced at him, wondering if

he'd been in town all day, or if the news had spread so fast that he'd come running from the home range. Then he lifted down the McClellan and set it upright.

'Whatever it is you've a mind to do,' rasped Baylock, 'ferget it.'

Now a challenge came into Will's eyes. 'If it was *your* wife,' he asked mildly, 'would *you* forget it?'

Ignoring that, Baylock said, 'You listen to me, Hooper, an' you listen good. Me an' you, we've never seen eye to eye, an' likely never will. But you take my advice. Goin' after the man you say defiled your woman won't change a damn' thing, 'cept mebbe turn a wife into a widow.'

'Save your breath, Baylock,' Will countered grimly. 'We both know you don't want me to go after the de Benedictus boy because you do business with his father. Well, too bad. Now, if you've finished, you can get the hell out of my road.'

'I *ain't* finished.'

'Then spit it out. I'm burning daylight, listening to you.'

Without taking his unpleasant blue eyes off Will's taut face, the rancher reached into his heavy pea jacket and pulled out a thin wad of twenty-dollar bills, held together by a small but fancy money clip. 'Don't go ridin' off after that boy,' he said. 'Stick around town awhile, buy your woman somethin' pretty to take her mind off her troubles.'

He threw the wad so that it landed at Will's feet, and beneath the clipped, reddy-brown moustache, his gash of a mouth formed into a cool, knowing smile.

Will looked down at the folded bills. He figured there must be at least ten of them. Two hundred dollars. He bent and picked up the money clip, weighed the bills briefly in one hand. Then, after an eternity, he said, reasonably, 'I got a better idea. You go on up to Camp Lincoln and take a good, hard look at my wife. You see for yourself what that sick little bastard did to her. And when you're all through looking, you offer *her* the money.'

He threw the money clip back with sudden fury, and it hit Baylock in the chest. Instinctively he reached up and clasped it to him, and in his anger, the skin pulled even tighter across his skull.

'You should'a took the money an' walked away from it, Hooper,' he hissed. 'Cause now I'm gonna make sure you ain't in no fit state to go chasin' off on your fool's errand.'

The cowhands who'd been flanking Baylock stirred and came forward, and Will backed away from them, having known all along that it would come to this. He thought briefly about the gun in his pocket. He hated to use it. When a man used a gun, things turned ugly, fast. But he wouldn't stand much chance going at it toe-to-toe, not against three of them.

He made a grab for the weapon, but the hammer snagged on the flap of his pocket and before he could bring it into play, they were on him.

He folded like a leaf in a cloudburst, and for a moment all was total confusion until someone grabbed him by the arms, pinned them tight and hauled him back onto his feet.

He knew what he could expect next, saw the other two bully-boys advancing with their fists cocked even as the thought seared across his brain. They were going to beat him so bad that he wouldn't even be able to sit a horse, much less ride for the Rio.

He could not allow that to happen.

Quickly, viciously, he brought his right foot up and slammed the heel of his heavy plough shoe back against the shin of the man who was holding him, kicked again and then gouged the heel down the length of the man's shin for good measure. With a howl, the man's grip slackened and Will shrugged out of it, but his moment of triumph was short-lived, because one of the other bully-boys lunged in and caught him with a roundhouse right to the jaw.

He staggered sideways, into the arms of the other bully-boy, who rough-handled him around and pinned his arms again. Cursing, knowing he mustn't let them have their way, he tried to stamp this cowman's feet, but then the first one came in from the front and punched him right in the belly.

Will groaned breathlessly and little balls of light popped in the darkness behind his screwed-shut eyelids. Another punch impacted against his ribs and he went up on his toes, still cursing.

Then the cowboy who'd doled out all the punishment stepped back a little to admire his handiwork, and that was a mistake. It gave Will a chance to drag down a fresh breath. And when Baylock snarled, 'Hit him again,' and the cowhand stepped back in to do just that, Will was ready for him.

He lashed out with his right leg, and the toe of his brogan slammed into the man's crotch. The cowhand keened out a high, womanly scream, hunched up, clutched himself and fell away, and at the same time Will used the only other weapon available to him right then: he brought his head back in a sharp, savage butt, and felt it connect with the face of the man who was holding him.

This man, too, gave a yelp of pain, but there was outrage in him as well, and instead of relaxing his hold the way Will had expected him to, he tightened it and screamed nasally, '*Get* 'im, Chester! Get the bastard!'

One of the bully-boys was still rolling on the floor, jack-knifed up and cupping his crotch. But that still left the other, and he came in like a twister. A fist exploded against Will's jaw, snapping his head sideways, and another buried itself up to the wrist in his belly, and after that the blows came even faster, so fast that after a while, Will could no longer tell them apart.

Then, above all the in-close grunting of the bully-boys, their laboured breathing and the flat, meaty thwack of knuckles connecting with his ribs, he heard a raised voice, sensed a sudden distraction in his tormentors which, for the moment at least, he was too damn' weak to take advantage of.

The voice snapped, 'What in hell you fellers think you're doin'?'

The bully-boy Will had kicked in the crotch had regained his feet by this time. Now he growled, 'Get the hell out of here, Lee.'

'The hell I will!'

Will raised his head and stared through the screen of his tumbled, sweat-slick fringe at a narrow-hipped man somewhere in his middle twenties, who had just come into the barn from the street and was slowly striding closer, his long, thin, weathered face registering shock. He, too, appeared to be a cowman, from the tip of his sweat-darkened, roll-brimmed Montana peak hat to the unbuckled shotgun chaps flapping loosely over his wash-faded blue denim pants.

'What the hell you think you're doin' here, Mr Baylock?'

Baylock rasped, 'It's Earl, ain't it? None o' your damn' beeswax, Earl. You get on back to the ranch.'

But the newcomer shook his head, and the lips beneath his straight, sun-peeled nose curled disdainfully. 'So's you can kill this here feller an' be done with it? Nuh-uh.'

Baylock cane-thumped closer, and when he spoke there was a scowl in his voice. 'I gave you an order, Earl. Now, you get out of here an' ferget what you've seen, or you draw your damn' time.'

Regret flashed momentarily in Lee Earl's darkblue eyes. 'I've liked workin' for you, Mr Baylock. You been hard, but you been fair with it. Still, I reckon I'd sooner quit than see you add to this sodbuster's misery.'

Without warning, Lee suddenly fisted the grips of his heavy, Schofield-modified Smith & Wesson .44 and Baylock and his plug-uglies froze before the handgun's deadly snout. A momentary silence filled the barn, and then Lee spoke again. 'Now, you get on out of here, all of you, an' leave this poor pilgrim be.'

The man holding Will snarled, 'You're bluffin'.'

Lee threw him a cold look. 'Why don't you try me, Bob?'

The seconds piled up into half a minute. Still breathing hard, Will wondered if this thing was going to come to shooting after all. But then Baylock offered Lee an unhurried shrug. 'All right, boy,' he said, peeling one of the twenties from the money clip. 'You're the one holdin' the gun. But you've burned all your damn' bridges around here.' He screwed the twenty-dollar bill into a ball and tossed it to the floor. 'Reckon that's about what I owe you. Take it and clear the county, *pronto*. Show your face in this bailiwick again an' I'll shoot it off, personal.'

For a further ten seconds he held

Lee's stare with a murderous one of his own, then turned and thumped off through the back of the corral, and reluctantly two of his bully-boys went after him, reluctant because their fighting blood was still up and they were anxious to settle this fresh account with the young cowhand. Finally Bob, the Baylock man who'd been holding Will by the arms, released his grip and shoved him forward so that he sprawled on his hands and knees.

Lee Earl waited until he too had gone, then released a long-held breath, stuffed his .44 back into its long, slim pouch and bent to reef up the crushed twenty-dollar bill. 'You all right, sod-buster?'

'Y-yeah.' As he dragged himself back to his feet, using the slats in the nearest stall gate like the rungs of a ladder, Will said, 'I'm . . . obliged to you . . . Mr Earl. It was . . . lucky for me that you . . . happened along.'

'Luck, hell,' Lee replied in that clipped, businesslike way he had. 'I been huntin' all over for you.'

Will's heavy breathing quietened abruptly.

'Heard what happened to your wife,' the cowhand explained. 'Heard you was goin' after the feller that did it, too.'

'I am. Baylock won't stop me.'

'Well, you're doin' a good thing, sodbuster, an' I wanted you to know it. That sonofabitch's been ill-treatin' women along both sides o' the border for too long.'

Will's mouth dropped in shock. 'You mean he's done this *before*?'

'Your wife weren't the first,' Lee replied gravely. 'An' you can bet your saddle she won't be the last.'

'She will, if I have anything to do with it.'

'An' I wish you luck. Jus' wanted you to know it.' Lee shoved the twenty-dollar bill into the pocket of his much-mended, waist-length denim jacket and studied Will critically. 'You look like hell, sodbuster. Best you get cleaned up afore you go about your business.'

Will touched his face. 'I . . . I'll do that.' Embarrassedly, he stuck out one hand. I really am obliged to you. Wish there was some way I — '

'Forget it,' Lee cut in impatiently, ignoring the proffered hand.

'But you lost your job on account of me.'

'I'll find another. You jus' move along afore Baylock an' them other fellers come back.' And so saying, he nodded a curt farewell, then turned and walked away.

★ ★ ★

The army surgeon, Dr Victor Gaines, was talking to Captain Peckover on the edge of the parade ground when Will rode in twenty minutes later. As soon as he reined back before them, the doctor answered the question that was written all over his anxious face.

'She's all right, Mr Hooper. Sleeping right now.'

Will's eyelids fluttered with relief as he swung down. 'Can I see her?'

Gaines shrugged. 'If you like. But you won't get much out of her. I've administered a potion of chalk and opium to help her rest. I figure that's what she needs more than anything else right now.'

'But what happened to you?' asked Tom Peckover, studying Will's battered face from beneath the brim of his chasseur forage cap.

'The law says it can't touch the man who did what he did to my wife,' Will replied tiredly. 'So I figure to go after him myself.' Seeing Dr Gaines stroke his sidewhiskers in obvious disapproval, he added quickly, 'Oh, I'm not after killing him, if that's what you're thinking. I plan to bring him back across the border to stand trial for what he did.'

'Someone disagreed with you, I take it?' said Peckover.

Will nodded.

'But you're still bound to go through with it?'

'If I don't, he'll do it again, and keep on doing it. My wife wasn't the first woman he's abused.' Turning his attention back to Gaines, Will asked, 'How long will she sleep, Doctor?'

Gaines pondered briefly. 'Certainly through till morning.'

'Will she be able to fend for herself when I get her home? I mean, I plan to do this thing quick as I can, but I'm not sure how long it'll take and . . .'

Exchanging a quick glance with the surgeon, Peckover said, 'In the circumstances, I think we could keep your wife in the infirmary for a week or so, if that would set your mind at rest. In fact, some of the officers' wives have already insisted upon it.'

Will's shoulders dropped. 'You people been real — ' he began, and would have said more, but suddenly it all caught up with him, and his throat tightened with emotion. All at once he could no longer speak, just bow his head and shake it slowly.

A long, uncomfortable moment passed, and then Peckover said gently, 'Why don't you go spend a few minutes with your wife, Mr Hooper?'

Will cleared his throat, sniffled wetly. 'I'll, ah . . . ayuh, I'll do that. Thank you, Captain.'

★　★　★

By the time Will left the infirmary, evening was giving way to full dark and it was too late to start after de Benedictus, much as he wanted to, so he decided to head back to the farm, get some rest and start out fresh in the morning. Though he was exhausted by the time he reached home, however, he was too keyed-up for sleep. And in any case, there were still plenty of chores to keep him occupied. He milked Sally, threw a scattering of dried corn to the chickens, dragged the discarded supplies indoors and did what he could to clean up the house. Sometime after midnight he finally sank onto the bed and slept.

He woke early next morning, his muscles stiffening now as the punishment he'd taken from Baylock's thugs began to make itself felt, and pumping water into the galvanized kitchen sink, he washed, then put parched coffee on to boil and went outside, intending to see how the day was shaping up.

The minute he opened the door, a voice said quietly, 'Mornin', sodbuster.'

Will started and spun fast towards the speaker. In the chilly dawnlight he saw a man sitting astride a buckskin horse thirty feet away — and froze as he recognized Lee Earl.

The young cowhand reached up to touch the rolled brim of his dark Montana peak hat. 'Figured you'd still be here,' he said.

Recovering from his surprise, Will replied warily, 'Light and set. There's coffee boiling.'

Lee dismounted, leaving the buckskin

groundhitched. 'Sounds good. Best not tarry overlong, though. I estimate we got us a fair piece o' travellin' ahead.'

'We?'

'Thought you could use some company on the trail south.'

He brushed past Will and went into the parlour, where he swept off his hat and rubbed crooked fingers vigorously through his short brown hair. As he pulled out a chair and sat down, Will said from the doorway, 'You're heading south?'

'That's where we'll find him, ain't it? That de Benedictus cuss?'

Will nodded dumbly. 'Sure. But . . . don't take this the wrong way, Mr Earl, but what's your interest in all this?'

Lee said, a little aggrievedly, 'Jus' figured you might 'preciate some help. He ain't gonna come quietly, you know. And even if you collar him, you won't be able to watch him twenty-four hours a day.'

Weighing that, Will crossed to the

sheet-iron stove, poured coffee into two of the cups that had survived the Mexicans' visit and brought them across to the table. 'Sorry it's not stronger,' he said absently. Then, 'It's not that I'm ungrateful. I'm just not used to anyone offering help, that's all.'

'Well, could be you need more help than you realize, sodbuster,' Lee replied, taking his cup with a curt nod of thanks and blowing steam off the surface of the dark liquid. 'I mean, you know what Alesandro looks like?'

'No.'

'You know how to get to Nuevo Oro?'

Will shook his head.

'Well, looks like I got the advantage, don't it? Helped run some livestock down there one time, for Mr Baylock. We stayed 'bout a week, so I got to know the layout of the place pretty well. Could come in useful, that.'

'I was counting on catching up with Alesandro before he reached Nuevo Oro.'

'You'll never do that, not now. He's got too much of a head-start on you. No, sir. You want that sonofabitch, you're gonna have to snatch 'im right outa the nest.'

Will blew on his own coffee. 'I still don't see why you're getting mixed up in it.'

Lee's grin showed strong teeth. 'I got nothin' better to do. Lost my job savin' your worthless hide, remember?'

'There's more to it than that,' Will said quietly.

The cowhand sobered. 'Won't deny it. They's a gal, works at the Black Pearl Saloon. Nice gal, name o' Lucy Brown. Me an' her . . . we had what you might call an understandin'.'

All at once Will thought he understood why Lee had sought him out yesterday to wish him luck. 'Alesandro beat her, too?' he asked.

Lee nodded. 'Not as bad as he done your wife, but bad enough, I reckon. The feller he rides with, Ugarte, he gave Lucy's boss some money to keep her quiet, but Lucy ... ' He sighed expressively. 'Well, let's put it this way, sodbuster, she used to look real handsome, did Lucy. But not any more.' Silence settled between them. 'How's *your* woman, anyway?'

'Army doctor says she'll be all right. She's strong.' A new thought occurred to Will, and he said, 'How long you been waiting outside, Mr Earl?'

'A while. An' my given name's Lee. Got to thinkin' that Mr Baylock might come after you again, him bein' so all-fired set on stoppin' you goin' after Don Miguel's boy.'

Will had been so busy thinking about Jane and Alesandro that such a possibility hadn't even occurred to him. 'Seems I'm still beholden to you,' he murmured.

'I don't know 'bout that. But I'm offerin' my help, sodbuster. Up to you whether or not you take it.'

'I'll take it,' Will said impulsively.

Fifteen minutes later they rode south.

81

4

They reached the Rio Grande around the middle of the afternoon.

At that point, the river was just a sluggish flow of muddy brown water fringed with live oaks and cactus, bled thin by all the irrigation ditches the cattlemen had dug over the years, so their crossing was unremarkable. Lee swung down on the far bank and allowed his horse to drink at the water's edge, and following his lead, Will dismounted and did likewise.

'Been a while since I forked a horse,' he remarked, sleeving sweat from his forehead.

'Sore?'

'Uh-huh.'

'You'll get used to it,' said Lee.

And ten minutes later they were back on the move.

Mexico — leastways, this Mexican

border country — wasn't that much different to the terrain they'd just left behind them, mostly greasebrush-covered badlands punctuated here and there by stands of cypress and Joshua, with low, powder-blue hills and golden, flat-topped mesas just visible in the extreme distance.

They rode on through the super-hot afternoon and made camp in a stand of paloverde trees just as the sky began to darken. Will broke out some of the supplies he'd taken from the farm and cooked a meal of dry salt meat and navy beans over a low fire. While Lee attacked the food with enthusiasm, Will just pushed his portion around his tin plate.

Lee watched him for a while, then said, 'Not hungry, sodbuster?'

Will glanced over at him. 'Just thinking.'

' 'Bout your woman?'

'About what's up ahead of us. How we're going to play it.' He paused a moment, feeling the weight of the

Peacemaker in his pocket, then set the plate aside. 'Might come to shooting, you know.'

Lee shrugged his careless shrug. 'I done a little of it before. You?'

'Not since the war.'

The war, he thought. He'd been lucky to come out of it whole. God knew, there'd been plenty fellers who hadn't, especially at Chickamauga, where more than half his regiment — Company A, 5th Georgia Volunteers — had been killed or wounded. A lot of enemy soldiers hadn't come out of it either, if it came to that, some of them because of Will's skill with a .577 Enfield carbine, and that still troubled him.

'Well, we'll try an' do it as peaceable as we can,' said Lee. 'But that Don Miguel, he's gonna be after us p.d.q., minute his boy turns up missin'.'

'We better make sure we give ourselves a good head-start, then.'

'Take the bastard after dark,' Lee decided. 'That'll give us the whole night before anyone misses him.'

'We don't want to get too close to the house if we can help it,' Will countered. 'Better if we snatch him outdoors.'

Lee gave another shrug. 'What about Ugarte? That feller, he's like Alesandro's shadow, always with him.'

'I owe Ugarte. Wasn't for him, my wife'd be dead now. But if we got no choice, we'll take the pair of them, worry about what we're going to do with Ugarte later.'

Lee nodded and, seeing Will wince, set his plate aside and rummaged in his plunder bag, finally bringing out a green-glass bottle that sparkled in the low firelight. 'Here,' he said. 'Might ease your aches some.'

Taking it, Will asked, 'What's in it?'

'Salt water'n whiskey.'

'I drink it?'

Lee chuckled. 'You rub it on your backside, you crazy sodbuster! It's the best damn' skin toughener there is.'

* * *

The next three days were more or less identical to that first one. Each morning they were up with the sun and riding ever deeper into Mexico, forever taking care to avoid every town, farm and stagecoach way-station they came to in order to keep their presence south of the border a secret. Will also kept one eye on their back-trail, just in case Baylock, knowing of his intentions, decided to come after them. But as near as he could tell, the big rancher had decided to stay home.

Four days later, as they refilled their canteens at a shallow rock pool midway along a steep-walled ravine, Will asked Lee how far he figured they were from Don Miguel's spread now. Glancing up, Lee said, 'We been ridin' across it all day, sodbuster. 'Fact, we ride extra careful from now on. Don't want to run into none o' Don Miguel's hands iffen we can help it.'

Hearing that, Will took a quick, guilty look around, the heady mixture of dread and determination reaching a pitch inside him as he tried to decide exactly how they were going to pull off what amounted to a daylight abduction. 'How far is Don Miguel's house from here?' he asked.

Lee jerked his head, chin-first. 'Mile or so t'other side of yonder ridge, as memory serves.'

Will nodded. 'All right,' he muttered grimly. 'Let's go find ourselves some high ground nearby. From now till we get our hands on Alesandro, we don't let that place out of our sight.'

* * *

Don Miguel looked up from his paperwork and called, 'Come.'

The door opened and Rafael Ugarte came inside. 'You sent for me, *jefe*?'

The Don nodded a silvery-grey head and gestured to the chair on the far side of his desk. 'Sit down a moment, Rafael.'

Meekly, Rafael did as he was told, but the big, pock-faced major-domo looked distinctly uncomfortable in the sun-washed finery of Don Miguel's combination office and study. He was a servant: he had no place in this big, book-lined room, with its ornate stone fireplace and fine paintings and sparkling crystal decanters filled with the rarest and most expensive sherries.

Sitting ramrod-straight behind the stack of ledgers, tally-books and correspondence that occupied most of his days, Don Miguel, by contrast, looked the picture of confidence and power. In his early fifties, he was a tall, fit-looking man, wide of shoulder, slim of hip and long through the legs.

'I am worried, Rafael,' the don said softly. 'About Alesandro.'

Back-lit by the white sunglare that bleached the billowing lace curtains behind him, Rafael saw only his silhouette, but well he knew the long, lined face, the high cheekbones, the hooked nose, the faintly bleak line of the mouth beneath the clipped moustache that was, like the brows that arched above his shrewd, nut-brown eyes, the same grey colour of storm-heads gathering above the Sierras.

Rafael shook his head. 'I do not understand . . . '

'Ever since you came back from America last week, he has been somehow . . . different. A different boy. Quiet. Frightened, almost.' The shrewd, nut-brown eyes came up to Rafael's face. 'Something is troubling him, Rafael, I know this. I thought perhaps he might have said something to you . . . ?'

Rafael shook his head some more, and hoped he sounded convincing when he said, 'Not a thing, *jefe*.'

'Did anything happen while you were away? Any trouble?'

'No, *jefe*.'

'You are *sure*, Rafael?'

'*Si, señor*,' he lied.

Don Miguel smiled tiredly. 'It's just that . . . you know how much he means to me, Rafael. When I am gone, all of this will be his, and to rule it well, to rule it *wisely*, he must have a clear head. His troubles, his worries, they are mine, too.'

'I would tell you if there were anything to be worried about, *señor*,' Rafael assured him. And that was another lie.

He, too, had noticed just how withdrawn Alesandro had become over the past week. Quiet, moody, scared. That business with the *gringo* woman had affected him more deeply than he cared to let on, for he had risked much — *everything* — submitting to his lust the way he had. And even though he felt safe enough now that he was home, confident that there was nothing to link him to the rape, and that even if there were, neither man nor law could touch him here because his father was big enough and rich enough to protect him from almost anything, he was still haunted by what he had done.

For Rafael, however, the opposite held true. He did not so much feel guilty for what he had done, but rather for what he had *not* done.

Leaving the woman alive, that had been a mistake. While she lived, she was a threat to his master. But he had been trapped in an impossible position. There was no way he could have pulled the trigger on her. No way.

Still, that one act of mercy in an otherwise merciless evening might well prove to be the undoing of Alesandro.

His one hope was that the woman and her man would say nothing, the woman because of shame, the man because he was, apparently, of little account in those parts, just a farmer stuck in the middle of cattle country.

Well, he thought. A man can hope. And pray.

Finding himself dismissed, Rafael closed the door behind him and went back through the cool house, with its whitewashed walls and red-tiled floors covered with rich, gaily-coloured rugs, and was just striding across the wide, flag-stoned courtyard, at the centre of which a fountain spat water into the air in a fitful, silvery arc, when a voice behind him called, '*Hola*, Rafael.'

He turned, surprised and vaguely unsettled to find Alesandro lounging in the shade of one of the whitewashed arches on the far side of the courtyard. Pushing himself away from the wall, the slender young man swaggered out into the sunshine.

'*Jefe*,' Rafael said respectfully, clapping his hat back on.

Alesandro threw a curious glance at the house. The don had fetched in Mexico City's finest architect to design it and oversee its construction, and wanting to protect his investment, had ordered a stone wall ten feet high and two feet thick to be built around it. Consequently, the place had always reminded Alesandro of a castle, and truly the *rancho* was a kingdom unto itself. Once the stout oak gates were shut and bolted, the ranch and the rolling, timbered hills beyond might as well be a thousand miles away.

He said, 'You have been talking with my father?'

'*Si, jefe*. He sent for me.'

'Why?'

'He is worried for you, *jefe*. He thinks you have been too quiet since we returned from the border.'

'And what did you tell him?'

'Nothing. Just that you were tired from the journey.'

Alesandro's near-black eyes had a dangerous, heavy-lidded quality to them that Rafael had seen before and hated. 'I hope that *is* what you told him, *compañero*,' he said quietly. 'I would hate to think that you had told tales out of school.'

'You know me better than that, *jefe*. Besides, what could *I* tell your father?'

Alesandro's white teeth flashed in a brief grin. 'That's right,' he said. 'You're as guilty as I am, aren't you?'

Rafael bowed his head miserably.

'Well, my father was right,' said Alesandro. 'I *have* been quiet. And it *is* out of character. I have been away, *amigo*, up here,' he said, and tapped his forehead. 'But now I am *back*.'

Rafael tried to look pleased to hear it. But inside, his disappointment was a painful, crushing thing. For the past few days Alesandro had been a good boy, a hard-working, polite, *good* boy. But as he had known all along, that wildness, that reckless disregard for others, it ran deep in his nature, and could not long be denied.

As the younger man turned and swaggered off, he thought sadly, *Si*. Alesandro is back. And, crossing himself swiftly, he murmured, 'May God help us all.'

★ ★ ★

Rafael had been right. That night at the farmer's place had scared Alesandro bad. But after a while, it had gotten so that Alesandro didn't think about the fear any more. All he remembered was the pleasure.

And *what* pleasure!

94

He had always loved the *señoritas*, to curse them and beat them and force them into submission. It was no good when they pretended, though, like the *putas* in Tacambaro and Mata Negras. He hated that feeling of pretence, that he was not really indulging his own particular tastes at all, just acting them out.

Ah, but the *gringo* woman . . .

For days he had not even dared to think about her, because this time . . . this time he knew he had gone too far. Never again must he be so reckless. But last night he had dreamed of her, seen again her sun-reddened face in his mind: her face, that was, after he had finished with it.

God, the pleasure she had given him, fighting him the way she had! The whore, she had made him curse her and beat her and throw her to the floor and take her! But she had paid the price for leading him on. He had beaten her to within an inch of her worthless *gringo* life, and then

95

Rafael had finished her for good.

Now that the mood was on him again, however, he began to wonder what it would be like to have killed her himself.

All at once his face, still marked faintly by the scratch-marks where she had fought him, clouded. He had missed a golden opportunity there. He saw that now. But he was sure he would discover the thrill of murder for himself, one day soon.

Soon.

All at once the restlessness was back in him. He could not cloister himself away here on the ranch, just waiting to become a copy of his own father! He wanted — no, he *needed* — fun: a woman; preferably a woman like the *gringo* whore, who would fight him every step of the way, and so increase his pleasure a thousandfold. And who knew, he might even finish her off himself, this time. After all, why should Rafael have all the fun?

The thought made him laugh. But

almost immediately he scowled again. *Rafael*. Once, he had been a good and trusted companion. Now he was more like a mother hen clucking around her brood, forever frowning and worrying and thinking of others.

Alesandro knew what he would say, when he announced his intention to visit Mata Negras for a few days. *You promised, Alesandro! You promised you would be a good little boy!* And deep down, he knew that was exactly what he *should* be.

It would be better, then, to visit Mata Negras alone. And why shouldn't he? He was no longer a child. Let Rafael sit at home and worry about silly, inconsequential things. He, Alesandro Larraya de Benedictus, was going to have *fun*! Perhaps the ultimate fun . . . .

Reaching his bedroom, he closed and locked the door behind him and crossed hurriedly to the closet in the corner. Tearing open the door, he dropped to his knees and rummaged inside for a moment. At last, from far back in the cupboard, he brought out a shining, factory-new .44 calibre Army Colt seated in the holster of a fine, hand-tooled, black leather gunbelt.

For a long, heavy moment he stared down at the gun, his breath quickening. He had bought it in secret several months earlier and hidden it away so that no one knew he owned it. At the time, he hadn't really understood why he'd wanted his own gun, not when he had Rafael to fight all his battles for him. But now, as he remembered Rafael going back into the farmer's cabin, as he heard again that single, deafening gunblast and imagined the bullet smacking into soft white flesh . . . now he knew why.

He chuckled softly.

It was settled, then. He would go to Mata Negras, alone, perhaps on the morrow. And, he told himself as he slid the handgun from its holster and caressed the smooth, cool metal lovingly, he would paint the town red.

★ ★ ★

For three days and three nights, Will
and Lee took turns watching the great,
whitewashed house from the cover of a
rocky outcrop barely a quarter-mile to
the south. For three days and three
nights they witnessed the comings and
goings of hired men, horses, wagons
and the occasional visitor. Once, Lee
pointed out a tall, regal-looking man
with silver-grey hair and said, 'That's
the Don.' But of Alesandro or Rafael
there was no sign.

It was a tense, edgy period — more
tense and more edgy than either of
them had expected — for they both
knew only too well that they could not
continue their fruitless surveillance
indefinitely. The longer they occupied
this jagged thrust of high ground, the
more likely they were to draw the
attention of Don Miguel's men. And
when that happened . . .

But Will tried not to think about that.
Instead he thought about Jane, what

she'd been through and why Alesandro must pay for what he'd done. And somehow that made the waiting easier to bear.

In fact, he was thinking about Jane, wondering how well she was healing and hoping she wasn't fretting too much about him when, mid-morning of the fourth day, Lee suddenly barked, 'Sodbuster!'

Will hurried over to the rim of the drop.

'There's our man,' Lee said softly, and pointed through the scrubby tangle of brush in front of them.

Hunkering beside him, Will saw that three figures had appeared in front of the big house beyond the huge stone wall. Don Miguel he knew, thanks to Lee. The big man with the broad shoulders and barrel chest could only be Ugarte. Which meant that the third man, the tall, slender man who was dressed immaculately in a waist-length tobacco-brown corduroy jacket and matching flared pants, was the man they'd come all this way to capture.

His jaw muscles bunched ominously.

Ugarte, he saw, was holding the reins to a big, charcoal-grey stallion while Alesandro and his father carried on some kind of animated conversation. Will frowned at that. If he didn't know better, he'd have said they were arguing about something. After a time, Don Miguel threw up his hands as if in defeat, ran one of them through his silver-grey hair and then, shaking his head, turned and disappeared into the house.

Alesandro reached for the horse's reins and Ugarte passed them across to him, grudgingly, it seemed. They too held some sort of discussion. Rafael appeared to be asking for something. He pointed away to the east, where the Benedictus horse-barn was located, but Alesandro made an angry, cutting gesture, slid one foot into the long, *tapadera*-covered stirrup and swung aboard the stallion.

'Looks like he's going someplace,

don't it?' murmured Lee.

Will nodded. 'All by himself, too,' he added, dry-mouthed.

At a signal from Rafael, two hired men drew back the huge wooden gates and Alesandro spurred his horse out onto the rutted trail beyond at a fast, northward gallop.

Lee hissed, '*Come on!*'

Catching up their own horses, Will and Lee hurriedly made their way down through untidy spills of grey, brown and dull red boulders until they reached the scree-filled ravine below. They still didn't have any definite plan in mind, just figured to pull ahead of their quarry and get the drop on him when he least expected it.

On level ground at last, they mounted up. Lee took the lead, because he knew the country and Will didn't. They followed the ravine north until it yielded to a gentle slope covered in hardy Jeffrey pines and, at the lower elevations, a sweeping belt of piñons, then cantered on for a further ten minutes, Will, a poor horseman, constantly struggling to keep up. At length, Lee drew rein and stabbed a finger away to their right. Breathing hard, Will drew down beside him and looked in that direction. Far, far below, beyond all the screening timber, he just about discerned Alesandro galloping his stallion along a trail that bisected the woods.

'We're gonna get that sonofabitch, sodbuster,' Lee gritted, bright-eyed with excitement now. 'We're gonna *get* him.'

Will nodded, pulses hammering as he scanned the land around them. 'Keep going, Lee,' he gasped after a moment. 'We'll pull out ahead of him, be waiting for him when he reaches yonder bend.'

Glancing down towards a distant point where the trail swung lazily north-east, Lee cried, '*Yee-hah*!' and all at once they were back on the move, the horses' hooves gouging great chunks out of the grassy slope as they pulled ahead of the young Mexican, then started dropping ever lower on a diagonal course that would bring them right to the edge of the trees.

Reaching the timberline, Lee hauled in again and while his buckskin shook its big head and blew hard through flared nostrils, he drew his modified Smith & Wesson .44 and checked the loads. Will slowed his chestnut to a halt beside him and tugged his own Peacemaker from the deep pocket of his coveralls.

'You ready for this, sodbuster?' breathed Lee.

Glancing at Lee's handgun, Will said, 'Yeah. Just don't use that thing unless you have to.'

Lee snorted. 'You think I want to bring Don Miguel's men runnin'?' He hefted the weapon. 'This thing's strictly for show, believe me.'

They backed their horses into the trees and waited, hardly daring to let the trail out of their sight now. Gradually their breathing calmed and the skittish horses finally settled. But when, after ten minutes, there was still no sign of Alesandro, Lee hissed impatiently, 'Where the hell's that sonofabitch gone to?'

In fact, Alesandro had reined down a short distance back in order to take his coiled gunbelt from his saddle-bags and buckle it around his slim waist. He was still smarting from the argument he'd had with his father about going to Mata Negras alone, too. *Dios*, if he hadn't known better, he'd have thought his father didn't *trust* him on his own!

Still, he'd won in the end. Adopting a sense of outrage, emphasizing his age and need for independence, these were the things that had finally won the debate. Not that his father had liked it much, even then. *You are an important man. Alesandro. You need protection.* And Rafael: *Please, jefe, let me come with you? If anything were to happen to you . . .* .But his mind was made up, and after a while, they'd seen as much, and resigned

105

themselves to it.

All of which meant that now . . . now, Alesandro had his chance to go to Mata Negras alone and enjoy himself without worrying about his father or Rafael or anyone else, not even the whore he intended to abuse and then kill.

Kill. The prospect alone made his throat go tight, and as he finished buckling the gunbelt, he saw that his long, artistic fingers were trembling faintly with anticipation.

Settling the weapon-heavy holster more comfortably on his hip, he heeled his horse back into motion, determined to waste no more time. But no sooner had he rounded the next wide, lazy bend than two men — two *gringos* — suddenly pushed out onto the trail ahead of him.

'Haul rein, you sonofabitch!' bawled Lee, stabbing his Smith & Wesson out at arm's length. 'You hear me? *Parada, hijo de puta!*'

Taken by surprise, Alesandro obeyed at once and brought the stallion to a spraddle-legged halt barely thirty feet away. His near-black eyes shuttled warily from one unfriendly face to the other, and he quickly concluded that he had never seen either man before. But their intentions, he told himself, were plain. They planned to rob him. And the fact that neither man wore a mask meant that they probably intended to kill him, too.

For one frantic moment he thought about turning the horse around and riding back the way he'd come, but they would shoot him for sure if he tried that. No . . . no . . . it would be better to co-operate with these men, give them whatever they asked for. He didn't want any trouble, and opened his mouth to babble as much. But even as he started raising his free right hand, he suddenly became aware of the handgun sitting on his right hip.

'Hands *up*, you little bastard!' snarled Lee.

Alesandro licked his twitching lips. If he could kill these two *ladrones*, would that not prove once and for all to his father and Rafael that he was a man full-grown? A man to be reckoned with? And was not killing a man almost as pleasurable as killing a woman?

A voice inside his head said, *Yes*, and in the following moment of madness he made his move.

Seeing it, Will yelled, '*Lee!*' But Lee was already way ahead of him.

The Smith & Wesson roared and a .44 slug smashed Alesandro in the left shoulder and threw him backwards out of the saddle. Even as he fell, though, he brought the Army Colt up and his finger jerked at the trigger. The gun bucked against his palm and one of the *gringos* — the one who dressed like a *vaquero*, the one who had shot him — cried out, hunched up and grabbed his right arm.

Alesandro hit the ground then, screamed high at the pain that tore through his shoulder. His stallion, made panicky by the gunfire, turned and bolted: he rolled sideways to avoid the driving hooves; and then he was back on his feet, wreathed in yellow dust, cursing these *gringo* bandits, bringing the Colt up for another shot —

From the back of his sidestepping chestnut, Will screamed, 'No!' and fired the Peacemaker reflexively.

The .45 calibre bullet punched Alesandro in the crotch, that one part of his body which had dictated every foul deed for which he was responsible, and a pain that was beyond description erupted inside him. He rose up onto the tips of his fine, hand-stitched, black-leather boots, fired the Colt one final time into the ground, staggered a bit and then spun around and collapsed.

For one horrified moment Will stared at him, watched as he squirmed in the dirt. As if from a great distance he heard Lee shouting at him through clenched teeth. After a moment he looked across at the other man, his gaze still vague and shocked, and seeing it,

Lee made a quick, irritable gesture with his good arm.

'*I said ride, you crazy sodbuster!*' he yelled. '*Lessen you want to hang, we gotta get us the hell outa here, right this minute!*'

5

With a muttered curse, Don Miguel threw down his pen and pushed himself away from the cluttered desk. How could he concentrate on book-keeping so soon after he and his son had exchanged such bitter words?

Shoving to his feet, he dry-washed his long face irritably. Then, with a heavy sigh, he crossed the study and poured himself a half-glass of sherry. All right, Miguel, he told himself wearily. Calm down, now. Perhaps the boy does have a point. Perhaps he should be allowed more freedom. But Don Miguel had always been protective — perhaps overprotective — of his son. His wife, his beloved Eleonora, had died giving birth to the boy, and her death had made Alesandro's life all the more precious to him.

Still, as Alesandro himself had

pointed out so vociferously that very morning, he was twenty-five years old now: old enough to take care of himself. And though one part of Don Miguel recognized that, another part — the part that knew all too well his son's shortcomings but chose not to acknowledge them — said that he would not rest until Alesandro was safely back home again.

Feeling tired beyond his years, Don Miguel took his glass across to the ornate stone fireplace, above which hung a portrait of his late wife. As he looked up into her serene face, the full, dreadful weight of his loneliness suddenly bore down on him, and he thought, almost painfully, *Ah, Eleonora, how I wish you were here with me now.*

It was just then that he heard the faintest flurry of what sounded like gunfire in the far distance, but by the time he reached the open window behind his desk it was gone. Even so, he propped there a moment longer, just

112

listening, but heard not even the echo of an echo. Finally, with a thoughtful sip at his sherry, he told himself he must have imagined it, and turned back to his desk, determined to get on with the day's business.

He was still poring over his tally-books when, several minutes later, a horse clattered into the courtyard outside, and one of the hired men gave a startled shout.

With a frown, he rose and returned to the window just as Alesandro's charcoal-grey stallion galloped by, the split-ended reins flapping loosely around its big head.

The horse, he saw, was riderless. And as Don Miguel recalled the gunfire he thought he'd heard earlier, something distinctly unpleasant suddenly wrenched at his innards. All at once he spun and ran from the room, through the house, out into the paved court-yard, his thinking growing ever more panicky. Something had happened to Alesandro. He *knew* it!

Bursting out into the full sunglare, he saw that one of the hired men had caught the horse's reins and brought the animal to a nervous halt thirty yards away: saw also that the distraught animal was wall-eyed and flecked with foam from its hard run.

Don Miguel felt the blood leach from his face.

'*Jefe?*'

He had just reached the horse when Rafael appeared at his shoulder. He glanced at the big major-domo and saw his own fears mirrored in Rafael's big, pocked countenance. For a moment he did not trust himself to speak. In any case, the sudden, dramatic appearance of the horse told its own story. At length, however, he managed a breathless, 'Something has happened, Rafael.'

Apparently Rafael had already reached the same conclusion because, with a grim nod of agreement, he barked at the hired man, 'Umberto — two saddle-horses, *now!*'

Moments later the big house grew

small behind them as he and Don Miguel pushed their mounts hard along the trail. They had barely gone a mile, however, when they spotted another of the Don's riders galloping towards them from the opposite direction, the brim of his big sombrero fluttering madly in the slipstream. Don Miguel immediately drew rein, and Rafael followed suit.

As the *vaquero* reined in before them, he called urgently, 'A wagon, *jefe! Por Dios*, I must fetch a wagon!'

Don Miguel shook his head, as if to clear it. 'What — ?'

'It is Señor Alesandro, *jefe!*' the *vaquero* gasped, pointing back the way he'd come. 'He has been shot!' And now, for the first time, they saw the tears in his eyes.

Don Miguel repeated in a shocked kind of whisper, 'S-shot?'

The *vaquero* bobbed his head and started to ride around them. '*Ahora, con permiso, jefe*, I must fetch a wagon! Without it he will never survive the journey back to the *hacienda*!'

★ ★ ★

Don Miguel dispatched a man to fetch the doctor from Mata Negras, and the married men whose wives knew something about fixing wounds were hastily summoned to the big house. While they did what they could for his unconscious son, the Don paced the wide hallway outside his room, trying not to think about the state in which they had brought his beloved Alesandro home.

'I just don't understand it, Rafael,' Don Miguel sighed with a shake of the head. He was still trying to make sense out of it all, and finding it impossible because he was still in shock. 'Who would do such a thing, and why?' He turned and paced back past the closed bedroom door, glancing at the blank panels as he did so, hearing some of the women in there muttering prayers, one of them wailing. 'Estevan says Alesandro mumbled something about two *gringos* when he found him.'

'Perhaps he was delirious, *jefe*,' Rafael suggested, hardly daring to look at his master.

'Or perhaps he was trying to tell us who had shot him,' Don Miguel countered. He spun on the bigger man so fast that Rafael jumped. 'And that's another thing. Why was he wearing a pistol? Where did he get it from?'

'I had never seen it before today, *jefe*.'

'No. And from the looks of it, it had never been *fired* before today.' Again the Don shook his head in bafflement. 'Perhaps he was expecting something like this to happen. Perhaps that is why he went armed. But then, if he was expecting trouble, why was he so determined to go to Mata Negras alone? None of it makes sense.'

He continued pacing for a while, trying to put all the pieces together in a way that fitted until, suddenly, he recalled the conversation he'd had with Rafael the day before, and thought again about what Alesandro had tried to tell the first man to find him.

'Rafael,' he said carefully. 'Are you *sure* there was no trouble while you were in America?'

'*Si, señor*,' Rafael murmured guiltily.

But this time, Don Miguel saw right through him. 'There's something you're not telling me,' he grated.

Rafael shrugged and shuffled and held out his big hands all at once. 'It might be nothing, no more than a coincidence,' he said quickly, the words falling over themselves in their hurry to leave his mouth.

'I will be the judge of that!' snapped the Don.

Rafael hesitated momentarily, then said, 'There . . . there was a woman, *jefe*. A *gringo* woman . . . '

And with a peculiar mixture of dread, relief and pure, wretched misery, the big man told him everything.

As the timber fell behind them, the country ahead opened out into a great, undulating sweep of grassland and gravel, occupied only by wandering beeves bearing the Benedictus brand. The cattle scattered lazily as their horses slipped and slid down into the shallow valley, leaving a churned trail that even a blind man could follow. But even as they bottomed out, Lee toppled sideways from the saddle, hit the ground with a bounce, rolled and then lay still.

Will, seeing it happen from the corner of his eye, quickly reached across and grabbed the reins of Lee's horse, brought both animals to a halt, turned them around and trotted them back to where Lee lay unconscious. Dismounting, leaving the horses ground-hitched, he grabbed his canteen and dropped to his knees beside his companion.

'Lee? Lee!'

After a moment Lee stirred and squinted up at him. His long, thin face was chalk-white, his dark-blue eyes slightly glazed. As he tried to rise, the pain in his arm made him hunch up and cry out. A moment later, panting hard, he croaked, 'What the . . . hell you doin', sodbuster? We gotta keep . . . movin' . . . '

'You're losing more blood than you can spare,' said Will, cradling his head and spilling water between his dry lips. 'I've got to stop it before we push on.'

Choking a bit on the liquid, Lee said, 'Can't spare the time for that . . . '

'We can't afford *not* to,' said Will. 'Now hold still.'

With a grimace, he took a Russell Barlow clasp knife from his pocket and opened it up. Then, as gently as he could, he cut the blood-soaked material of Lee's denim sleeve away from the wound. As near as he could tell, Alesandro's bullet had gone right through, shattering the elbow joint on

120

its way out. The pain, he thought, must be awful.

Glancing around in a vague, detached manner, Lee said, 'Wh-where are we, anyway?'

Will shrugged. 'I don't know.' He took out a kerchief, spun it into a manageable length and tied it just above the wound. Then he slid the knife through the loose knot and turned it gently so that the kerchief gradually tightened around Lee's arm.

'Damn you, sodbuster!' Lee gritted. 'We ain't got *time* for this! We . . . gotta ride!'

'Hush now, and save your strength,' Will replied, easing off on the tourniquet for a moment, then tightening it again.

When the blood had slowed to a sluggish ooze, Will shoved the clasp knife away, untied and wet the kerchief with water from the canteen and did his best to clean the puffy, faintly blue entry hole. Lee's teeth clamped hard and, after a few moments, his eyelids fluttered weakly and he slipped back into unconsciousness.

At length Will tossed his blood-soaked kerchief aside and released a heavy sigh. The amiable cowhand was right, of course. They *did* have to keep moving. But Lee was too weak to ride. This time he'd been lucky: the next time he fell off his horse he might well break his neck.

For one fleeting moment a sense of hopelessness threatened to engulf Will, but he thrust it aside and busied himself binding the wound with Lee's own bandanna. By the time he was through, Lee had regained a hazy kind of consciousness, and reaching a snap decision, Will helped him climb to his feet and then boosted him back into the saddle. While Lee sat there, swaying gently back and forth with his chin resting on his chest, Will rummaged through one of his saddle-bags until he found a pigging string. With this, he tied Lee's hands to the horn of his saddle, to hold him in place.

The job done, he remounted and

took Lee's reins in his free hand. Now all he had to do was get them the hell out of here. But that was easier said than done. Lee was the one who knew these parts: he, Will, didn't have a clue. Sagging again, and cursing his own inadequacy, he tried to bring order to his thoughts.

As long as they kept heading north, they would eventually reach the Rio Grande, what they called the Rio Bravo on this side of the line. But which way was north? He glanced at the sky and tried to judge direction by the position of the sun, but so much had happened in such a short space of time that he still couldn't think straight. After a moment he settled on a direction he believed — hoped — to be north, and got them back on the move.

★   ★   ★

Sometime around late afternoon he forced himself to stop fretting about what had happened to Alesandro and what might still happen to him and Lee, and threw a tired glance skyward. The sun, he saw, was now well behind them, throwing their shadows long across the inhospitable terrain ahead.

Behind them.

With a sudden stab of alarm, he reined in quickly and his lips moved in a silent, *Oh God, no.* If they were headed north, the sun should have been away to their left by now. Which meant . . .

The breath left him in a harsh, ragged hiss. *Which meant that, instead of leading them to the safety of the border, he'd been leading them east, away from it.*

Despair threatened to crush him. How could he have been so stupid? But then, he'd had a bad feeling about this ever since he'd got them back on the move: he'd just been too distracted to really think about what he was doing.

Leaving the grasslands behind them sometime around noon, they'd entered a weathered rock- and tree-filled arroyo, and he'd frowned at that, because he had no memory of having passed that way on the journey south. But still he'd kept them pushing on in the same, hopelessly wrong direction until the winding contours of a vast, rocky canyon clustered with garambullo and great, beaked yucca had taken them even further off-course. The seamed land had started to rise in a series of broad folds and sweeps after that, and now, ahead of them, it shelved towards the deep blue sky in a series of ragged peaks and craggy plateaux, their topmost contours lost in a faint, misty heat-haze.

Brushing insects away from his sweaty face, he hipped around and briefly considered retracing their route. But what if Don Miguel's men were already after them? To go back would be to deliver themselves right into the Don's hands; to continue pushing forward, by contrast . . .

He turned his green eyes back toward the jagged, talus-covered slopes, stippled here and there with blind prickly pear and clusters of yellow paper flowers.

To go forward meant having to cross the mountains.

He glanced at Lee, who was slumped in his saddle, dozing, his hands still tied to the horn. Flies were crawling all over the bloodstained bandanna tied around his arm. Lee would doubtless know what to do, but Lee was in no position to offer advice right now.

Again Will looked at the mountains, mouth dry, guts churning, the hands fisted around their reins quirky and unsteady.

There was, he thought, no help for it. They had to go forward.

Heeling the horses back to a canter, he led them desperately on into the shadow of the towering peaks.

* * *

Don Miguel spent the rest of that long day in his study, brooding over what

Rafael had told him. At first he had slapped the big man across the face and called him a liar, because Alesandro, his precious Alesandro, would never do the things Rafael had said he did. Rafael had tried to protest, of course, but seeing the fury in Don Miguel's eyes, had quickly fallen silent.

No. Rafael had simply mistaken the events he had described. This *gringo* woman, she had obviously identified Alesandro as someone of breeding and wealth, and doubtless led him on. Rafael himself had admitted that she was as poor as a church mouse. Why shouldn't she try to sell her charms for a few dollars? When Alesandro had refused to pay her for her favours, however, she had evidently concocted a story and sent her foolish man on his dreadful errand.

By the end of the afternoon he had convinced himself entirely that this was the case. He would not allow himself to think anything else.

The ornate clock on the mantelpiece

had just finished chiming the hour — six o'clock — when there was a soft rapping at the door. The sun had dropped behind the *hacienda's* thick, protective walls by this time, and the room was bathed in a soft, smoky orange glow.

Don Miguel, sitting behind his desk, rose slowly and said, 'Come.'

The door opened and a tall, thin-bodied woman in her late thirties — Umberto Casaravilla's wife, Rosanna — came inside.

For one charged moment nothing happened. And then, very softly, the Don breathed, 'He is dead, isn't he?'

Rosanna Casaravilla nodded tearfully and quickly stuffed a bunched handkerchief to her mouth and nose. 'We did all that we could, *jefe* — '

Reaching out to steady himself against the edge of the desk, the Don nodded and said, still speaking in that strange, lifeless half-whisper, 'Tell Rafael I would see him.'

The woman turned and left him

staring up at the portrait of his late wife.

A few minutes later Rafael knocked at the study door and was told to come inside. The big man entered hesitantly, turning his big hat nervously in his hands. But Don Miguel was no longer angry with him, for now they were united by their loss. The Don looked at him through the building gloom, saw the paleness of his face, the salt-water soreness of the eyes beneath his heavy brow, and said gently, 'You have heard the news?'

Rafael nodded.

'Go to the bunkhouse and tell the men,' the Don said tonelessly. 'And while you're there, send another rider to Mata Negras. He is to tell the *jefe de rurales* there that two *gringos* have murdered my son. Tell them we do not know why, but that we suspect robbery. While he is there, he is also to post a reward of five thousand pesos for the capture of these men — alive.'

'*Si, señor.*'

'And Rafael? Pick the ten best men we have and tell them that we will be riding after the killers ourselves at first light. Tell them we will hang these *asesinos* from the nearest tree for what they have done.'

'Jefe — '

'Do it, Rafael!'

Rafael dipped his head. '*Si. jefe.*'

'Now,' said the Don, brushing past him, 'I go to say goodbye to my son, and swear vengeance in his name.'

★ ★ ★

Will led them up through the gentle, grassy foothills until the vast, exposed slope suddenly turned even rockier and steeper. Then he reined in and looked up at the seemingly insurmountable barrier that lay before them, and it was like seeing it, *really* seeing it, for the first time.

Stretching away to north and south, the incline thrust toward the sky in a bleak, weather-worn tilt of chunky grey rocks and, here and there, patches of prickly pear and chino grama grass. From this angle, the peaks and plateaux he'd seen earlier looked more unreachable than ever: their scored granite tips seemed almost to scratch the very sky itself.

Again, briefly, he thought about turning back, but knew it was too late for that. So — they climbed.

Even following a faint deer-trail, the going was hard. And because the best route to the top lay in a series of broad, sweeping zig-zags, it slowed them to a crawl and quickly sapped the energy of horse and rider both.

The sun nestled on the horizon behind them and threw long, cold shadows across the lonely slopes ahead. Once, twice, three times, the trail, such as it was, just petered out, and Will was left seeking an alternate route. After a while he decided that it was probably easier to dismount and lead the horses by their reins, though his clumsy brogans weren't made for climbing and he slipped and fell more times than he could count. Soon his cut knees ached and bled, his deep-scratched palms itched and stung. But gradually, gradually, the incline began to level off.

And that was when it happened.

Will's horse stepped on a small, loose rock that suddenly shifted under his weight, and the animal stumbled, lost his footing and started scrambling madly to regain his balance. Will, at the other the of the reins, was suddenly yanked backwards, down the slope, and all at once they were lost in a cloud of dirty, yellow-grey dust and the horses, both of them, were screaming and panicking and kicking up miniature landslides of pebbles.

Digging his heels in and hauling back on the jumping reins, Will yelled something, he didn't know properly what, and away to his right, aboard the prancing buckskin, he saw Lee coming round, crying out at the pain in his arm and bawling a high, startled question about what the hell was happening.

Too busy to tell him, Will continued fighting desperately for control of the horses. But the chestnut had been nervy all the way through the climb, and now that he couldn't seem to regain his footing no matter how hard he tried, he was pulling ever more frantically on the reins in Will's fist, as if breaking loose would somehow help him.

Will yelled, '*No . . . no!*' But even as he cried out, he felt the reins slipping inch by inch through his sore palms. He yelled again, '*No . . . no . . . no!*' and dug his heels in deeper, willing the chestnut to settle, praying for the strength to hold him steady.

But there was only one way the drama could end, and that was the way it *did* end.

The chestnut gave one final, backward wrench of his big head and the reins tore free of Will's desperate grip. And in the very next moment, as Will tumbled forward onto his knees and quickly transferred his grip to the buckskin, the chestnut collapsed on his flanks, flailed at the early-evening sky with his forelegs and then spilled sideways with enough force to bust his ribs. Screaming high, like a woman, he rolled, twisted and went tip over tail back down the slope, legs snapping like brittle twigs, muscles tearing, every bone in his wiry body cracking and punching jaggedly up through his flesh.

Then the chestnut was gone. And so were most of their supplies.

Will croaked weakly, 'No . . .'

Slowly, warily, the buckskin began to settle.

'What the . . . what the hell we doin' here, sodbuster? Where the hell are we?'

As he dragged himself back to his feet, Will said woodenly, 'Long story.'

'Then you better get started tellin' it!' raged Lee.

Will, trembling like a leaf, only looked at him. 'Later,' he said, then turned and started them climbing again.

How long it took them to reach the top, he had no idea. Realistically, it was a matter of hours. To his desperate mind and bone-weary body it seemed more like days. But all at once he realized that they were working their way through a forest of boulders and copal trees, and the ground underfoot was as near to level as it was likely to get.

As the sun dropped lower, plunging them into an eerie purple twilight, he collapsed, gulping down great draughts of cool air, shivering and sweating all at once. After a while he said, without looking around, 'How do you feel?'

'Lousy,' husked Lee. 'I'm still waitin' to hear that story, too.'

Will surveyed their surroundings in the fading light. To his surprise, he saw the remains of a small, tumble-down village clinging to the slopes about a quarter-mile to the south. The small, square adobes, among which peculiar cone-shaped structures had been built from coiled grass and mud, were in a poor state of repair: in all likelihood, they'd probably lain abandoned for more than a century.

Sleeving his face, he gathered up the reins and led them on, towards the dwellings. Along the way he told Lee what had happened. At first Lee swore hard, but then fell silent. Twenty minutes later he untied Lee's hands, helped him dismount and half-carried him into the most complete ruin, then off-saddled and quartered the buckskin in the roofless building next door.

While Lee tried to settle himself more comfortably in one corner, Will struck a lucifer and examined the single, featureless room in which they had ended up. Old bones, picked-clean corncobs, fragments of pottery and little shaped lengths of wood that might once have been knife-handles, littered the floor. He gathered up as much of this fuel as he could and built a small fire in the opposite corner.

'It's been a hell of a day,' he muttered at length.

'I don't recall much about it,' Lee said groggily.

'Well, I'm sorry it's worked out the way it has, Lee. Truly.' He gestured to Lee's arm. 'I'd better clean that up and splint it. Then we'll see about fixing some food.'

Working by the fitful light of the small fire, Will untied the bandanna and peeled it away from the wound. The elbow joint looked fat and swollen, possibly infected. As he did what he could for his companion, he asked softly, 'You ... you reckon I killed him?'

Lee winced. 'A-Alesandro?' He pondered for a moment, then said, 'I reckon. Don't figure they's too many men'd walk away from a wound like that 'un.'

Will's head bowed a little, and he said in a small voice, 'Wasn't meant to work out like that, was it?'

'What're you belly-achin' about?

You got what you wanted, didn't you?'

'I wanted justice, Lee, not vengeance.'

Lee shook his head in disgust. 'Christ Almighty, what is it with you? Who cares what you call it? The sonofabitch got . . . what was comin' to him, di'n't he? That's all that . . . matters.'

'I didn't want to kill him.'

'Well, you did, so that's an end to it,' Lee spat harshly. He stared at Will for several seconds, then said, 'You know your trouble, sodbuster? You spend too much time bein' sorry for everythin'. It's like you've had all the get-up-an'-go punched out of you.'

That brought a sudden, unaccustomed surge of anger to Will, because he knew that what Lee had said was the absolute, unvarnished truth. 'It was men like you who did the punching, Lee,' he bit back. '*Cattle*men. And don't keep calling me sodbuster!'

'Then start actin' like a man,' Lee

growled. 'We're in a hell of a fix here — sodbuster. The hell with de Benedictus. He's history. We gotta think about ourselves now, an' how we're gonna get outa this mess.'

In the distance, a bobcat screamed at the moon.

6

Will didn't think he'd sleep much that night but he did, and it was pretty close to dawn when he stirred again and sat up, feeling cold and hungry. Lee, he saw, was still hunched in the corner behind the door, shivering and hugging himself one-armed against the morning chill. In the colourless dawnlight, the young cowhand looked more like a corpse.

Climbing quickly to his feet, Will unscrewed their canteen, held it to his lips and asked gently, 'How d'you feel?'

'Like h-hell,' Lee replied, shivering as he swallowed some of the liquid. 'Damned arm feels like it's on fire, rest of me feels like ice.'

Nodding, Will untied the bandanna, which was stiff and filthy by now, and studied the wound with a grimace. Lee's arm had swollen to twice its normal size, and pus had collected in and around the bullet's entry-hole. It smelled foul.

'We got to get you to a doctor,' he said at last.

Lee snorted weakly. 'Better think again, s-s-sodbuster.'

'I mean it. You don't get that wound seen to soon, you'll lose the arm.'

For just a moment Lee looked very serious and very afraid. Then he licked his lips and shook his head. 'I can wait,' he gasped. 'Let's jus' get us outa this . . . lousy country first, huh?'

'I don't think you can wait that long, Lee.'

'Look, jus' — '

Abruptly Lee clamped his mouth shut and stared at his companion with wide, urgent eyes. Will stared back at him and nodded, for he too had heard a faint rustling of movement outside.

Thrusting up away from his companion, he ripped his .45 from the pocket of his coveralls and thumbed back the hammer. But, as he ghosted over to the

141

small, glassless window on the far side of the door, the very last thing he expected to see — a herd of about thirty goats — suddenly ran, walked and trotted into view. They were being hazed along by a pot-bellied, bare-headed Mexican in the usual off-white shirt and *pantalones* of the lower classes. A young boy, carrying a long stick, was hurrying along beside him. From his size, Will estimated him to be no more than nine or ten.

'It's a *goat*-herd,' Will called over one shoulder.

With effort, Lee rose to his feet. 'A *what*?' And then, as Will shoved his Peacemaker away and reached for the doorhandle, 'Hey, now — '

Will looked at him. 'You need help, Lee. Maybe this feller can tell us where we can get it.'

'Hold on a minute, you loco — !'

But it was too late: Will had already dragged the sagging door open and stepped outside.

No more than forty feet away, the

goat-herd and his young companion pulled up sharp and stared at him fearfully. As goats milled around his legs, Will raised his empty hands and called, '*Buenas dias.*' It was about all the Spanish he knew. 'Please, I mean you no harm. It's just, my friend and me, we . . . we need help.'

The goat-herd, a short, stocky man with a heavy red face, looked at him blankly. Then Lee stumbled into the doorway behind Will, and the man's dark eyes fairly saucered.

'*Ayuda,*' Lee called impatiently, pointing to his arm. '*Estoy indispuesto. Me duele el brazo.*' He glanced at Will and hissed, 'Got any money on you?' And when Will nodded, Lee called to the goat-herd, 'We can pay.'

Licking his lips, the goat-herd breathed, '*Tu es proscrito? Muy mal hombres?*'

Lee shook his head tiredly. '*No. Justo desgraciado.*'

'What's he saying?' asked Will.

'He th-thinks we're outlaws.'

'And what did you tell him?'

'I said we've just been unlucky.'

The goat-herd rattled off some more Spanish then, and pointed back the way they'd come. Sweating now, Lee said, 'He says there's a little village about three, four miles south-east of here, an old man who knows s-somethin' 'bout medicine, speaks American, too. He says the boy'll take us there.'

'See? What did I tell you?'

Ignoring him, Lee bobbed his head at the goatherd and said, '*Muchas gracias, mi amigo. Muy agradecido.*'

With new heart, Will hurriedly saddled the buckskin, gathered the remains of their gear together and helped Lee to mount up. Ten minutes later, while the wary goat-herd continued to push his flock north, his boy led the two *gringos* in the opposite direction, towards a town he called Concepción.

★ ★ ★

'This is a bullet wound,' said the old man, inspecting Lee's arm through a flimsy pair of thumb-smudged glasses. 'How did it happen?'

It was a little over two hours later, and the boy had led them down through the mountain passes to a whitewashed sprawl of buildings which sat uneasily upon a bleak but gentle slope facing brush- and scrub-covered flats away to the east. A fistful of stores and a small church had been built around a central plaza, very much in the Mexican fashion, and the smaller, meaner *jacals* of the *peones* had clustered in crooked rows behind them.

As they approached the town, Lee had asked the boy if they had any law down there. To his relief, the youngster had shaken his head, then guided them on through the town and across the busy square where, it seemed to Will, inquisitive *peones* stopped and watched them every step of the way.

On the far side of the plaza they stopped at a small, peeling adobe set between a boarded-up store and some kind of mercantile. Here the boy thumped at a heavy door until an old man came to answer it. The old man looked from Will to Lee, the alert brown eyes behind his spectacles lingering on Lee's arm while he listened frowningly to the boy. Finally, speaking in very good English, the old man told the two Americans to come inside. Before the boy could take his leave of them, Will gave him a silver dollar from the money left over from the sale of his wagon and, with Lee translating, asked him to board the buckskin at the nearest livery.

As he closed the door behind them, the old man told them his name was Felix Paesar and that he wasn't a real doctor, though he had studied many fine medical tomes in his youth. Doctoring was his hobby, he said. Before retiring, he had been a baker, a very good one. He was in his late sixties now, a little stooped, with wiry iron-grey hair and a clipped beard.

Indicating that Lee should sit up on the edge of a table that was stacked with books and newspapers, he commenced his examination. 'How did this happen?' he asked almost immediately.

'Does it . . . matter?' growled Lee, alternately sweating and shivering.

'I am just curious,' said the old man, disarmingly.

'I shot a man who was . . . sh-shootin' at me,' Lee winced. 'Satisfied?'

Paesar nodded. 'Ah. So you are a *pistolero, si*?'

'I'm a . . . cowhand, mister.'

'And yet you go around shooting people?'

'He had it coming,' said Will, speaking for the first time.

The old man glanced at him. 'You killed him, then, this man?'

'That wasn't the intention,' Will said irritably. 'We — ' He broke off suddenly and stabbed a finger at Lee's arm. 'Look, just fix him up, will you?'

'*Claro, claro.*' Paesar sucked air through his small nostrils, then said to

147

Lee, 'I must reopen the wound in order to drain the poison. Then I must clean it, I mean really *scrub* it, to stop the infection from returning. Mmm . . . There is much splintering of the elbow, too. I will remove what fragments I can and patch up what is left.'

'It'll be . . . all right, though, won't it?' Lee asked shakily.

The old man looked a little surprised by the question. '*Señor*,' he replied regretfully, 'I doubt that your arm will be of much use to you ever again.'

A heavy silence descended over the small room.

'*Now, con su permiso*,' said Paesar, holding up a surprisingly delicate pair of hands, 'I go to wash up.'

As he left the room, Will swallowed hard and said, 'Lee — '

But Lee, pale-faced, shook his head. 'Ferget it, sodbuster. Wasn't none o' . . . your doin', jus' my lousy luck. Still, I figure this is gonna . . . take a while. Best you go buy yourself a fresh horse. Supplies, too. We still got a heap o'

. . . travellin' ahead of us, remember.'

Will nodded and said unhappily, 'I'll be back soon as I can.'

★ ★ ★

True to his word, Don Miguel led Rafael and a posse of ten vengeance-hungry *vaqueros* away from the big house at first light. Among them was a surly fellow named Fausto Talon, who had Yaqui blood in him and could, they said, read sign the way other men read books. Talon rode out ahead of the main party, and when Don Miguel and his riders left the timber behind them some time later, they found him standing beside his speckled mustang, waiting for them.

As the Don reined down and his men clustered behind him, the half-breed held up a bloodstained kerchief. He was short and bow-legged, with a thin face, a hooked nose, a sour mouth and shaggy black hair that stuck out from beneath a big sombrero.

Don Miguel took the kerchief and cocked his jaw, wondering what to make of it. A moment later, casting the rag aside, he barked, 'Ride on!'

The Don had sat with Alesandro all night, holding one of the dead boy's hands in his and asking himself why such a thing should have happened. Alesandro, he had told himself, was a good boy, a fine son. He should have lived a long, full life and given his father many grandchildren. But for this lying *gringo* whore and her stupid man, he would have, too.

At length he had planted a soft kiss on Alesandro's cold forehead and left the room. Retiring to his own quarters, he had then washed, changed, taken his own weapons belt from a wardrobe and buckled a single-action, .38-calibre Lefauchex pistol around his slim waist.

He was sure that the killers would make for the Rio Bravo by the most direct means. In other words, due north. But he had never been a man to leave much to chance, and as an afterthought he had instructed Rafael to seek out Fausto Talon. As it turned out, that was just as well, for a few miles further on, Talon signalled another halt, slid down from his low-horned saddle and studied the ground, eventually jabbing one stubby finger off to their right.

Don Miguel squinted in that direction. East? He could think of no good reason why the assassins would wish to head east. Unless, of course, they were trying to shake off any pursuit.

Again he said, flatly, 'Ride on.'

Three hours later they drew rein in the shadow of the looming mountains and, after a few moments spent scanning the rocky slopes, the Don's shrewd, nut-brown eyes snagged on a strange, bronze-coloured shape about halfway to the top.

Pointing, he said to Rafael, 'What do you make of that, *compañero*?'

Rafael, who had wanted no part of the manhunt, narrowed his eyes briefly, then said, almost unbelievingly, 'It is a horse, *jefe*. The body of a horse.'

A tight, unpleasant smile passed across Don Miguel's mouth. 'So,' he muttered. 'One wounded, and one a-foot, yes?' Hipping around to face his sweating followers, he made a quick overarm pass and called fervently, '*Vamos, hombres!*'

And with a jab of the heels, he sent his magnificent palomilla horse up toward the foothills.

* * *

Felix Paesar whispered, 'Shh, now. Your friend is sleeping.'

As Will stepped into the peeling adobe and the old man closed the door behind him, he saw that Lee was seated in a rocking chair beneath a small, half-open window, sunken eyes closed, narrow chest rising and falling slowly. The wound had been rebound in a clean white bandage, he noted, and the arm itself was resting in a sling tied around Lee's neck.

'How — '

'Shh.'

He followed the old man across the room and through to a small kitchen, where the baker-turned-medic poured him a mug of very welcome coffee. 'You can use this I think, *si*?'

Setting his gunny-sack of recently purchased provisions aside, Will took the mug with a grateful nod. 'How is he?' he asked softly.

'He will sleep for a while, and when he wakes, his arm will *ache* for a while. But he will be all right, I think.'

Will swallowed hard. 'Thank — uh, *gracias*. What do I owe you?'

'*Nada*, my friend. Nothing.'

'Nothing?'

'Señor Earl,' the old man explained, 'told me everything.'

He took his own mug across to the small rosewood table that occupied the centre of the floor, flopped into a creaky ladderback chair and gestured for Will to take its companion. Around them, the kitchen was bright with sunlight, hot with the fierce noonday heat. 'Do not think he betrayed your confidence,' he continued. 'He spoke only after I had administered some chloroform to lower his guard and put him to sleep.' He added carefully, 'I wish your wife a good recovery from this business. Sincerely, I do.'

Jane. As Will took the seat, the ache in him to see her again was almost painful. 'We didn't mean for things to turn out the way they did,' he said. 'I mean, killing de Benedictus wasn't part of the plan.'

'So your friend told me. But as you yourself pointed out earlier on, that unholy demon had it coming.'

Will started. 'You know Alesandro?'

'Yes, we know him here in Concepción,' said the old man. 'Him and his father. Don Miguel took and hanged two of our fine young men a couple of years ago, for stealing one of his cows.' He snorted bitterly. 'What did it matter to him that the cow had wandered far from de Benedictus land, that it was only one of tens of thousands that bear his mark, or that we here in Concepción had suffered a hard winter and the families of those same two men were close to starving?'

'And Alesandro?' Will prompted through set teeth.

Paesar curled his whiskery lips. 'About a year ago he and his bodyguard paid us a visit. I don't know why. Perhaps Alesandro had grown bored with his usual haunts. Anyway, while he was here, Alesandro saw a girl who caught his eye and tried to . . . how would you say it? He tried to court her, *si*? But when she refused his advances, he lost his temper and beat her so savagely that he shattered her pelvis. Sixteen years old,' he said, 'and crippled for life.' After a pause he added, '*Si*, he had it coming, as you said. And that is why I treat your friend free of charge.'

Will fell silent for a moment, shocked to the core. Then he asked, 'When will Lee be able to ride?'

The old man shrugged. 'A few hours.

Whenever the narcosis wears off.'

'It's just that we figure Don Miguel's bound to come after us.'

'Oh, he will,' Paesar agreed with chilling certainty. 'But do not worry, señor. I have already passed the word. If Don Miguel does turn up here, do not fear that my people will betray you. They won't. They owe Don Miguel nothing.'

Just then they heard Lee groan softly, sit up and retch.

Paesar was beside him in a flash. 'It is all right, Señor Earl,' he murmured. 'You are all right, now . . . '

Lee retched a few more times, then calmed a little. His dark-blue eyes, bloodshot and watery now, sought and found Will, standing in the kitchen doorway, and he croaked, 'You get yourself a . . . decent horse?'

Will nodded. 'Just give yourself a chance to recover and then we'll make tracks, all right?'

Paesar checked his pulse and temperature and asked him how he felt.

Lee said his arm throbbed like a bitch and his head didn't feel much better, but other than that, he was fine. Apparently satisfied that this really was the case, the old man hustled back into the kitchen while Lee dragged down a series of slow, deep breaths to chase the last of the anaesthetic away.

A short time later, Paesar returned with two bowls of watery chicken broth. As he handed one to each of his guests, Lee shook his head and said he didn't think he was up to food just yet, but Paesar insisted. 'You have lost much blood in the last thirty-six hours,' he pointed out. 'You must rebuild your strength for the journey ahead.'

To add weight to the argument, Lee's belly reminded him that here was the first food either of them had eaten since the night before, and anxious though he was to move on, he was suddenly equally anxious to satisfy his faintly sickening hunger. Without another word, he and Will wolfed the meal, and by the end of it a hint of colour had returned to Lee's thin, weathered face.

Thirty minutes later, the young cowhand pronounced himself fit enough to ride. He wasn't any such thing, of course, but it wasn't as if they had much choice in the matter.

At the door, the old man offered them his hand. 'I wish you could stay and recover at leisure,' he said. 'But I understand why you have to keep going.'

'*Muchas gracias*, Señor Paesar,' said Lee, shaking left-handed with him. 'I'm real beholden.'

'We both are,' said Will.

The old man waved their thanks aside. 'You are still about a hundred and fifty kilometres from the border,' he reminded them earnestly. 'That is what, a hundred miles? Maybe a little less. And the going is hard, every step of the way. But if you ride east from here, down to the flatlands below, then swing to the north and keep the mountains on your left, you will eventually reach the Rio Bravo.'

'We'll make it,' said Will. And he thought, *We've got to*.

It was siesta-time in Concepción, and the plaza was deserted as they headed for the only livery stable in town, a big, plank-built structure that was situated almost directly opposite Felix Paesar's humble dwelling. Lee shuffled along like an old man, but the improvement in his general well-being was plain to see. No sooner had they passed through the stable's big double doorway, however, than a faint, rumbling sound reached their ears, coming from the north-west.

They had just enough time to exchange one questioning glance before twelve riders galloped their dusted mounts into town.

Quickly stepping to one side of the doorway, Lee swore, and Will, standing right behind him, whispered, 'Don Miguel?'

Lee nodded. 'Yeah — and loaded for bear, too.'

Thinking fast, Will glanced around

the stable. The only occupants were a few horses standing boredly in their stalls and a few more milling around in a pole corral out back. The proprietor was nowhere in sight: doubtless he had gone home during this quiet, oven-hot time.

'I'll saddle the horses,' he said. 'Maybe we can slip out the back way.'

But even as he turned and started dragging his newly-acquired short-skirted Texas saddle down off the wooden tree just inside the doorway, Lee swore again.

'Hold up, sodbuster.'

'What is it?'

'Don Miguel's sendin' one of his men over this way,' hissed Lee, drawing his .44 left-handed. 'An' lessen I'm much mistaken, I'd say that it's Rafael Ugarte hisself.'

* * *

The climb had been a difficult and dangerous one, and Don Miguel's men had approached it warily and with no small reluctance. The Don himself, however, had shared none of their concerns. All that mattered to him was that he catch and hang the killers of his son. So what, if the mountains stood in their way? The *gringos* had managed to scale them. So would they.

Consequently, following much the same trail Will had taken the afternoon before, the Mexicans had dismounted and, leading their nervous horses by the reins, picked their way slowly, carefully, to the top. At one point — the worst, as far as many of the *vaqueros* were concerned — they had been forced to ascend right past the ruptured, fly-blackened remains of Will's chestnut. The horses hadn't cared much for that. But three hours later they'd finally topped out sweating, gasping, exhausted and almost indescribably relieved.

Don Miguel, apparently unfazed by the climb, had immediately dispatched Fausto Talon to scout ahead for sign, and doubtless would have followed straight after him had Rafael not suggested he call a brief halt.

Pausing with one boot in the stirrup, Don Miguel had frowned at him.

'The men,' Rafael said softly. 'We have pushed them hard today.'

Surprise showed briefly on the Don's long, aristocratic face. *Men?* He had been so intent on his mission that he had forgotten all about the men. Now, glancing around at them, seeing their weariness and the state of their horses, he nodded, ran the back of one shaky hand across his mouth and muttered distractedly, '*Si . . . si. Bueno.* Uh . . . tell them we move out again in thirty minutes.'

Fausto Talon came back long before then. He told Don Miguel that he had found signs where the *gringos* had slept in one of the old abandoned adobes barely a quarter-mile to the south, and that he had also found tracks to indicate that they had gone south-east, towards Concepción, earlier that very morning.

162

Don Miguel nodded slowly and ground his teeth in anticipation of the confrontation to come. Watching him, Rafael no longer saw his beloved master, but rather an older version of Alesandro.

'So,' said the Don. 'Why do you suppose they would head for Concepción, Rafael?'

Rafael shrugged. 'Supplies?'

'Perhaps. Or perhaps to find a doctor for the wounded man.'

Fausto Talon hawked and spat. 'There is a man in Concepción who has some understanding of medicine,' he offered quietly. 'His name is Paesar.'

'I remember the fellow,' said the Don, thoughtfully.

It was a short ride down through the hills to Concepción, and they galloped in a little after three o'clock. The town was empty, for this was the hottest part of the day, the part when sensible men, women and children holed-up against the fearsome heat. But as soon as they clattered into the plaza, the Don began issuing his orders.

'Pablo, Ramon, check out that cantina. Joachin, Eduardo, Maximo — ask after the *gringos* at those stores. Fausto, check the trail out of town for sign. Rafael?'

'*Si, jefe?*'

'Take a look in that livery. If you find a horse that looks as if it's been ridden as hard as our own, they are still here.'

'*Si, jefe.*'

The Don squared his shoulders. 'Now,' he grated, 'let the rest of us pay a visit to this man Paesar.'

* * *

Felix Paesar was in his kitchen, washing up the bowls his recent guests had left behind them when there came a loud and urgent hammering at his door. He turned, wondering if the *gringos* had come back for some reason, and hurried through his modest little house to open it.

His hand had just closed on the knob

when the man on the other side of the door suddenly kicked inwards, and Felix Paesar was thrown back across the room to fetch up hard against the edge of his cluttered desk.

'Que — ?'

Filling the doorway, Don Miguel jabbed a finger at him and snapped, 'Where are they?'

Felix Paesar straightened his glasses on his nose and suddenly the indignant creases in his forehead smoothed out as his face went slack with shock. 'D-Don Miguel,' he whispered.

The Don came inside and half a dozen big, gunhung *vaqueros* poured in behind him. He pulled up short when he smelled carbolic on the air, and something else, something sweet and noxious, like chloroform. 'Where are they?' he said again. 'The *gringos*?'

'I don't . . . '

One of the *vaqueros* came out of the kitchen holding a fistful of blood-smudged rags. 'I found these outside, *jefe*.'

'That blood,' said the Don. 'It is fresh?'

The *vaquero* nodded.

Don Miguel reached down, grabbed Paesar by the collar of his shirt and dragged him roughly to his feet. 'Tell me, old man!' he raged, and to the surprise of every man there, who had known the Don for years and respected him beyond words, he drew his .38 from its pouch and slammed it savagely across Felix Paesar's face. 'Tell me where the *gringos* are, or so help me, I will shoot you where you stand!'

7

'Looks like I'm gonna kill me a greaser,' Lee murmured grimly as Rafael continued to lead his tired horse toward the livery barn.

'A greaser, yeah,' Will agreed in a tight whisper. 'But you won't kill all twelve.'

'Got any better ideas?'

'We hide,' said Will. 'We hide and we pray like hell he doesn't find us and raise the alarm.'

Lee's mouth — whiskery now, like Will's — narrowed down. He'd never run from a fight in his life, and though he hated the idea of doing so now, he didn't argue the point because he knew that Will was right. The minute he gunned Ugarte, Don Miguel and the rest of his men would come a-running, and when that happened, they'd find themselves surrounded pretty damn' quick. On the other hand, if they could just get under cover before Ugarte reached the stable . . .

It was a long-shot, but without further discussion they backed away from the sun-filled doorway until they reached a crude wooden ladder about halfway along the central aisle, which led to the hayloft above. Then Will hissed, 'Come on, now, move it!', and Lee stuffed the .44 back into leather, put one booted foot on the first rung and, still moving like an old man, started climbing onehanded.

'Come on . . . come on . . . '

'I'm goin' . . . fast as I . . . can, dammit!'

But Lee wasn't even halfway to the top when the stable doorway darkened and Rafael planted his big silhouette, and the silhouette of his horse, right in the middle of the weathered frame.

Seeing Ugarte's arrival from the edge of his vision, Lee stopped climbing and turned a little at the waist. There was no way he could draw the .44 now, no way Ugarte could miss seeing them, either: and standing directly below him, at the foot of the ladder, Will's breathing grew heavy and urgent as he wondered where the hell they went from here.

Rafael's surprise at seeing them was momentary: then his mournful brown eyes dropped from Lee's face to the bandaged arm resting in the sling around his neck, from the arm down to Will, and when they came to rest on Will there was, strangely, a kind of recognition in them.

After a long beat, Rafael said quietly, in hesitant English, 'Señor Hooper?'

Will gave a slow, careful nod.

'Your wife,' said Rafael. 'How is she?'

'She ... ' Will cleared his throat, tried again. 'She's all right. No thanks to Alesandro.' Eyeing the bigger man more closely, he said, 'He died, didn't he?'

'He died yesterday evening.'

Will let his breath go in a soft rush. 'Well, we didn't plan to kill him,' he said. 'We figured to arrest him, take him back to America and make him stand trial for what he did to my wife, but the damn' fool went for his gun, didn't give us any choice.'

Rafael nodded sadly. 'I believe you, señor.' He threw a brief glance at Lee. 'You were just about to leave, si?'

'That was the idea,' growled Lee.

'Then go,' said Rafael, to their complete amazement. 'Ride swiftly and do not look back. I will do what I can to delay Don Miguel.'

Lee frowned. 'How come you' lettin' us go?' he asked suspiciously.

'What's done is done,' the Mexican replied with a lifeless shrug. 'Alesandro has paid for his sins. Let that be an end to it.'

And without another word, he turned and started back across the plaza, dragging his reluctant horse behind him.

'You reckon we can trust that feller?' asked Lee, watching him go.

All Will could say was, 'He did the

right thing by Jane.'

'Well,' said Lee, starting to ease himself back down the ladder, 'you heard the man, sodbuster. Let's saddle up an' get us the hell outa here.'

* * *

Rafael left his horse ground-hitched with the others outside Felix Paesar's adobe and, squaring his broad shoulders, shoved in through the open door.

The men who had accompanied Don Miguel were standing around the edges of the small, untidy room, each one looking distinctly ill at ease. In the centre of the room, pistol in hand, Don Miguel was standing over the old man, Paesar, who was down on his knees and bleeding from a short, deep gash in one cheek. He was, Rafael saw, trying to gather up the pieces of his shattered spectacles.

As Rafael came inside, Don Miguel kicked the little fragments of glass and the twisted wire frames from the old man's grasp, and they spilled across the puncheon floor with a faint, musical tinkle. 'I warn you, old man, no more of your denials!' snapped the Don. 'Where did the *gringos* go when they left here?' And to Rafael's horror, he swept the barrel of his pistol across the old man's face again, so that the foresight tore another ragged cut through his dry, parchment skin.

As Paesar cried out and fell sideways, Rafael stepped forward and put a restraining hand on the Don's gun-arm. '*Jefe, por Dios* — '

But he saw at once that the Don Miguel he knew no longer existed, that in his place stood a grieving father who would stop at nothing to find the killers of his son. The Don swore at him, shrugged him off and pushed him away, and then they stared at each other for a moment, until the bright, unpleasant light in Don Miguel's eyes faded.

'You have checked the stable,' the Don said at last.

Rafael nodded. 'There was no sign of them.'

'Well, they have been here,' breathed the Don. 'And this worthless cur has treated the wounded one, though he denies it.'

'Perhaps he is telling the truth, *jefe*,' offered Rafael.

'We have the evidence,' said the Don. 'Bloodstained rags, the stink of chloroform in the air, mugs and bowls that show he has had visitors here, and recently.'

'All right!' spat the old man, squinting up at him. 'The *gringos* you speak of . . . *si*, they *were* here. One of them had been shot in the arm. I . . . I asked them no questions, just tended the wound, and then they rode on.'

The Don dropped to his knees and grabbed Paesar roughly by one shoulder. 'That's more like it,' he grated. 'How long ago was this?'

'Three, four hours,' the old man lied.

'Which way did they go when they rode out?'

'East. But they will be . . . long gone by now . . . de Benedictus.'

Just then a horse cantered up outside, and a moment later Fausto Talon bow-legged his way inside. Rising, Don Miguel snapped, 'Well?'

The half-breed shook his head. 'I could not find their tracks on the trail out of town,' he said. 'I think they are still here somewhere, *jefe*.'

Don Miguel frowned. 'But the old man says — '

And then the room grew silent while Don Miguel looked down at Felix Paesar: Felix Paesar, the worthless *peon* who had dared lie to him.

The Don made a low, animal-like grunting sound deep in his throat and swung the pistol at Paesar's head yet again, but this time Paesar ducked beneath the blow and shuffled towards the door, first on his hands and knees, then pushing up onto his feet.

The Don screamed, '*Stop him!*' and snap-aimed his .38 at the retreating man's back, but again Rafael grabbed at

174

him, clamped one big hand around the Don's wrist and thrust the gunhand up so that the weapon discharged into the ceiling.

'*Jefe*, for the love of God — '

Pushing him away, Don Miguel yelled again, 'Stop him, you men! And you, Rafael — get out of my sight!'

*   *   *

Will had just finished saddling the ribby-looking paint pony he'd purchased to replace the chestnut when the single gunshot shattered the hot afternoon silence.

Lee, who'd been standing beside his own watered, grained and rested buckskin, murmured, 'What the *hell* . . . ?'

They reached the stable doorway just as Felix Paesar burst out of his little adobe and staggered straight into the arms of the other de Benedictus riders who had just converged on the place. One of them, hearing Don Miguel's shouted command, grabbed the old man, twisted him around and flung him toward one of his companions, who caught him and pinned his arms roughly to his sides.

Seeing the blood streaked across one side of Paesar's face, something inside Will suddenly hardened, like steel. A moment later Don Miguel himself strode out into the plaza, gun in hand, face like thunder. He stormed right up to Paesar and pistol-whipped his head sideways.

Lee growled, 'Sonofabitch,' and, left-handed, began to haul iron.

Beside him Will said harshly, 'Forget that. Mount up.'

'Hell with that! That old man fixed me up pretty g — '

'Just mount up, dammit, and make ready to ride!' hissed Will, and with a glare that silenced his companion he strode back to the horses, fisted the stock of Lee's scabbarded Winchester and dragged it free.

On the far side of the plaza, meanwhile, Don Miguel had seized

Paesar's sweat-and-blood-streaked face in his free hand. 'Do you know what they did to my son, these *gringos*?' he was asking. 'Huh?! Do you know what they *did*, old man?'

'Wh-whatever they did,' husked Paesar, 'y-you can be sure your son deserved it.'

Eyes widening in fury, Don Miguel raised his gun-arm with the clear intention of stoving Paesar's skull in, but even as his arm blurred up, the throaty boom of a long gun tore across the plaza and Don Miguel screamed out, dropped the .38 from nerveless fingers and grabbed at his numb right hand.

For one stunned instant no one was really sure what had happened. Then, as Don Miguel fell to his knees, Will pumped the Winchester's lever and fired again, and the man who'd caught and shoved Paesar to his companion was suddenly flung to the ground, where he screamed and grabbed at the fleshy part of his left leg.

All at once the other *vaqueros* started clawing for their guns, and Paesar, now forgotten, stumble-ran for the safety of his adobe. Inside the stable, mounted and holding Will's reins for him, Lee watched in astonishment as the sod-buster drew a bead and fired again, and another de Benedictus man dropped and started writhing in pain.

'Jesus, Mary an' Joseph — '

As spent shells flipped through the air still trailing smoke, Will squeezed off another shot, and a third Mexican staggered and fell. Then Will shifted aim, and lever-fired so rapidly that the deafening blast of five shots blurred into one. Whitewashed stone powdered and splintered off the facing wall of the boarded-up store outside which Don Miguel's riders had left their horses, and all at once the horses, spooked by the nearness of the gunfire, started backing up and wheeling around and running.

Will thrust away from the doorway then, threw himself into the saddle, tore his reins out of Lee's grasp and yelled, 'Ride!'

Following his lead, Lee jabbed his heels into the buckskin's flanks and they galloped down the aisle and out into the corral beyond, driving milling horses ahead of them. As angry bullets peppered the front of the stable, a rough-hewn pole fence suddenly appeared in their path, and seeing it, their mounts broke stride for one terrifying moment and then, with a great bunching of hind-quarters they leapt high, took the fence, came down on the far side with enough force to slam the air from their riders' lungs and then surged on across the gentle, scrubby incline that opened out in front of them at a hard run.

Carried away by the moment, Lee whooped at the top of his voice and yelled, '*Whoo-wee! Nice shootin', Will!*'

Will didn't make any reply . . . but silently he allowed that *Will* sounded a whole lot better than *sodbuster*.

That evening, sunset daubed the western sky with thick purple and gold streamers, but Felix Paesar was too busy to appreciate their majesty. There were wounds to tend: not easy when you no longer had your spectacles to help you.

Of the three wounded men, two had been shot in the leg, the third in the shoulder. In short, injuries calculated to incapacitate . . . But not to kill. For his part, Don Miguel had only sustained some light bruising to his right hand, caused when his pistol had been shot from his grasp, but Paesar had made as much out of the injury as he dared in order to delay any immediate pursuit of the *gringos*. He had fussed and clucked around the Don, bathed the hand, applied salve and bandage, and then suggested — respectfully, of course — a brief period of rest, to get over the shock.

As the long afternoon died and the

rest of his men went to find and catch up their scattered horses, the Don retired to Concepción's only cantina to nurse a cloudy drink and brood upon the events of the afternoon.

By their actions, the *gringos* had saved Paesar from almost certain death. More, they had stopped the Don himself from committing murder. They had scattered the horses to buy themselves time to escape and, by wounding his men, had given Don Miguel reason to spare Paesar — indeed, for the Don to put himself in the old man's debt.

Neither was it lost upon him that he had been at the mercy of the *gringo* who had done all the shooting. The man could easily have killed him outright and solved all his problems, but he hadn't. Perhaps he expected gratitude, for the Don to spare his life in return, when they finally came face to face.

Well, there was no chance of that.

Just then the cantina door swung

open with a weary creak and Rafael came inside. Stopping in front of the Don's corner table, he said, 'We have rounded up the horses, *jefe*, and the wounded have been seen to. The rest of the men await your orders.'

'And *you*, Rafael?' asked the Don, huskily. 'What about *you*?'

'*Jefe*?'

'Why did you tell me there was no sign of the *gringos* in the stable, Rafael? Why did you lie to me?'

Rafael opened his mouth, intending to say that the *gringos* must have been hiding when he checked the stable, but on impulse he opted for the truth instead. 'You are hunting these men for doing what any man would do in the same circumstances,' he blurted. 'And that is wrong, *jefe*.'

Beneath his thin grey moustache, the Don's lips squeezed down. 'Then you still maintain that Alesandro forced himself upon this *gringo* whore?'

'I was there, *jefe*. I *know* he forced himself upon her.'

'How can you even *say* such a thing! May God forgive you for the lies you spread about my son!'

'I speak only the truth, *jefe*, and we both know it. There was a . . . a sickness in Alesandro. But we do not always care to acknowledge that which is distasteful to us, so we look the other way and pretend that things, and people, are not really the way they are.'

Don Miguel came up out of his chair and slapped Rafael with his uninjured hand. In the confines of the dingy cantina, the blow sounded loud and strangely hollow, but there was enough force behind it to knock Rafael's big head sideways, and bring an ooze of blood to his lips.

'I should kill you for speaking thus about my son,' the Don said in a trembly kind of whisper. 'But instead, I banish you, Rafael. Do you hear me? I banish you from my lands and from this province. Go on, get out of my sight, and be thankful that I spare you your miserable life!'

'You perform no kindness in sparing me that,' Rafael replied, making no move to sleeve the blood from his mouth, 'for the life of a servant without a master is worthless.'

He turned then, strode to the door and let himself out into the carmine sunset, and it took all of Don Miguel's willpower not to call after him, *No, Rafael wait! I didn't mean it!*

As the cantina owner started lighting lamps against the coming night, the Don just stood there, listening to the sound of Rafael's horse carrying Rafael out of his life, after twenty-five years, for ever.

★   ★   ★

Frank Doyle, the sheriff of Camp Lincoln, was trying to catch up on some paperwork when he became aware of an angry babble of voices in the street outside. With a frown he rose from behind his desk, hitched at his gunbelt, settled his hat squarely atop his plastered-flat black hair and stepped outside.

Up on the opposite boardwalk, a sizeable crowd of men had gathered outside the offices of the town's semi-regular newspaper, the *Camp Lincoln Monitor*, there to purchase, read and, apparently, comment upon the latest edition. If the outrage in their raised voices was any indicator, however, whatever they'd read had sure gotten them riled up.

Scratching curiously at his thick, wiry beard, Doyle crossed the street and called, 'All right, fellers, simmer down now. What's the problem here?'

'This,' said a thin, slope-shouldered townsman named Pardee, thrusting a copy of the paper towards him.

Doyle glanced down at the headline, which proclaimed boldly:

CAMP LINCOLN MEN
ACCUSED OF MURDER!
MEXICAN RANCHER
SWEARS VENGEANCE
ON UNITED STATES CITIZENS!

With an oath, he snatched the paper and held it closer to his narrowed eyes. The first paragraph explained that what followed was a very rough translation of a three-day-old newspaper report taken from the Coahuila *Reportaje*, a much-travelled copy of which had come into the editor's possession earlier that same morning. The report claimed that two nameless *norteamericano* bandits had cruelly murdered the son of Coahuila's most respected rancher, Don Miguel Larraya de Benedictus, and were believed to be heading for the Rio Bravo, and the safety of their own country, in an attempt to escape the consequences of their 'cowardly' crime. The murder had been reported to the *jefe de rurales* at Mata Negras by one of the Don's riders, but it was understood that 'the grieving father' intended to take 'the dispensation of justice' into his own hands, since he had posted a 5,000 peso reward for the capture — alive — of the killers. The translation concluded with some strong anti-American hyperbole, and a closing editorial by Allen Prentice, owner-publisher of the *Monitor*, which hinted that Alesandro's murder was directly linked to his 'alleged' attack on the wife of 'a local farmer'.

'God *damn* that man Hooper!' Pardee said with feeling. 'He's goan spark off another war with Mexico, that's what he's goan do!'

'That's crazy talk!' yelled a man called Lyle Payne, who worked as a bartender at the Black Pearl Saloon. 'You'd've done the same thing yourself, iffen it'd been your woman.'

'Ah, don't hand me that!'

The bartender made a disparaging gesture. 'Oh, come on, now! We all know what that dirty little Mexican bastard was like!'

'That's just hearsay!'

'You tell that to Lucy Brown — iffen you can stand to look her in the eye.'

'Comes to that,' growled Doyle,

without realizing it, 'you tell it to Hooper's wife.'

All at once Doyle became the centre of attention — much to his discomfort. 'You takin' that sodbuster's side in this, Frank?' demanded a third towner. 'You sayin' it's all right for a man to take the law into his own hands now?'

'I'm saying I don't suppose we really gave him much choice,' Doyle replied gravely, knowing he shouldn't get involved but suddenly unable to stop himself. 'Because just when he really needed the law, and just when he really needed his neighbours, they weren't there for him.'

'So you're sayin' he did good, killin' that young Mexican?'

'I'm saying Hooper told me he figured to ride south and arrest the de Benedictus boy, and I believe that was his true intention. If it worked out that he had to kill him instead, well, I reckon he had his reasons. But I'd stake my life on the fact that he didn't murder Alesandro the way that Mexican paper'd have you all believe!'

'Damn' right!' agreed Payne.

'Now, break it up here,' Doyle finished gruffly, 'and move along before I charge you all with obstruction! And you, Pardee: no more talk of war, you hear me?'

As he turned and started back across the road, he saw Ned Baylock standing on the boardwalk outside his office, watching him. As he approached the big, ageing rancher, he nodded a short greeting. 'Help you, Ned?'

Baylock, leaning his full 200 pounds on the gnarled cane in his right fist, gave him a curious look. 'If I heard a-right, an' you was defendin' that damn' sodbuster jus' now, then it could be I need to help *you* — to come to your senses, Frank.'

Doyle was in no mood for a lecture. Looking into Baylock's long, weathered face, peculiarly pale but for two definite spots of colour on his gaunt cheeks, and hairless but for the thinnest, rust-red moustache, he said, 'You've read that garbage in the *Monitor*, then?'

Baylock gave him an emphatic nod. 'Always did say Hooper was a trouble-maker. Well, he's sure stirred up a hornets' nest this time, I reckon.'

'Maybe he has, at that,' Doyle agreed softly. 'But I'd as soon you didn't try to turn *his* misfortunes to *your* advantage, Ned.'

'What the hell does that mean?' Baylock demanded icily.

'Just that you never did cotton much to Hooper, and you might just see this business as your chance to get rid of him once and for all.'

'Huh. An' you'd stop me, is that it?'

'You know something, Ned? I do believe I would.'

Baylock sneered. 'You're gettin' soft in your old age, Frank.'

'Not soft, Ned, just sick. Sick of standing by and enforcing one kind of law for you, and another kind for Hooper. If I'd done my bit right at the start, he wouldn't be running for his life right now, his wife would have had her man beside her through some pretty rough times, and maybe Don Miguel's boy'd still be alive.'

'You finished?' Baylock asked tightly.

Doyle shook his head. 'I got just one more thing to say,' he replied. 'Just now, Lyle Payne told them other fellers that Hooper was only doing what any other man would do in the same situation. But he was wrong, Ned. I don't think there's another man in this town'd have the *guts* to do what Hooper did.'

'Hooper's a loser. A no-hoper. A *sodbuster*, fer Chris'sakes.'

'Hooper's got sand, and he's got principles. The rest of us? Hell, we just do whatever you *tell* us to do.'

'Jus' keep it up,' Baylock threatened in that low, gravelly voice of his. 'I ain't never see'd a man talk hisself out of his job before.'

Doyle's smile was cool. 'You just think about it, Ned. Hooper's a good man. A *strong* man. We ain't got too many of them in these parts, and we surely can't spare to lose any.'

He let himself back into his office and closed the door gently on the big rancher, leaving Baylock to stare after him with jaw muscles clenching. A moment later he gave an angry snort and thump-shuffled away, hardly able to credit that Frank Doyle would dare speak to him the way he had. But he'd have the last laugh on that burly bastard come re-election time, just see if he didn't.

Wrapped up in his thoughts, he stepped off the boardwalk without looking and shuffled right into the path of an oncoming Dearborn wagon. The first he knew of his mistake came when the driver dragged back on the reins and called out, *'Whoa, there!'*

For just a moment Baylock froze: then he twisted to face the small, light wagon as it bounced to a violent halt little more than a yard or two from him. Peering beyond the single team-animal, he was surprised to find Captain Tom Peckover sitting up on the seat: more surprised still to see Jane Hooper seated beside him.

'Better watch where you're going next time, Mr Baylock,' advised the tall, athletic-looking cavalry officer.

Baylock sucked air through his nostrils and hobbled slowly past the horse to the wagon itself. 'I was at fault, right enough,' he replied. 'Lucky for me you had such quick reactions.' He peered up at Jane and touched the fingers of his left hand to the brim of his hat. 'Good to see you up an' about again, ma'am. Whole town heard about your misfortune.'

'Is that what they're calling it?' Jane replied. She turned her very pale-blue eyes onto him then, and the hurt in them, the worry and sadness and the sheer, undiluted misery, stunned him for a moment. Wordlessly, Ned inspected the fading bruises around her puffy, bloodshot eyes, noted the swelling still present in her broken nose, the heavy bandage that kept her broken-but-healing wrist steady and the careful way she held herself so's not to put too much strain on her cracked ribs, and suddenly he felt a sharp stab of shame.

He looked at her and saw for the first time exactly what Don Miguel's sick-minded little boy had done, and he could hardly believe that he had tried to buy the sodbuster off with a lousy $200 when his wife had suffered all this. 'You, uh . . . you goin' back out to your place, now?' he asked uncomfortably.

Jane nodded slowly. 'Chores won't wait, I'm afraid,' she replied.

'No, I . . . I guess not,' Baylock rasped. 'Well, uh . . . don't let me delay you. I wish you well, Mrs Hooper.'

And quickly he turned and thump-shuffled away, hating the feeling of being ashamed: of being ashamed to the core.

8

'Dammit!' said Lee. 'They' still on our tail.'

'I see 'em,' Will muttered with a nod.

For three days they'd been following the mountains north, and as Felix Paesar had predicted, the going had been hard every step of the way. To the west lay rugged slopes littered with pitted grey boulders, mesquite, stands of acacia and thin, skyward-pointing saguaros. To north, south and east, the land alternated between vast, flat stretches of burning yellow sand, fringed with sickly green belts of cholla and brittlebush, and bleak, wrinkled areas scored through with twisting arroyos and scrubby, stunted trees. It was country calculated to wear a man down and, sure enough, it had quickly sapped what small reserves Will and Lee still had left. But up ahead somewhere lay the Rio Grande and, beyond it, the relative safety of America: and that was what kept them going.

Trouble was, Don Miguel was right behind them.

Now, while their spent mounts stood droop-headed beneath the hammering sun, Will and Lee scrambled up to higher ground and scanned their backtrail. Around them, the boiling afternoon was absolutely still, with not even the hint of a breeze, and there, high in the sky innumerable miles south, hung a lazy pall of saffron-coloured dust: dust kicked up by hard-pushed horses.

The Don's horses.

Lee swore with enough force to blister paint. 'What the hell does it take to shake that sonofabitch off?' he asked a little desperately.

With a shake of the head, Will rubbed a hand across his whiskery jaw. He, like Lee, had lost weight and condition: he'd grown sick of running, he was hungry, thirsty, tired to the bone, and he missed Jane more than ever. But he thrust all of that aside and focused his haunted green eyes on the distant, flea-sized riders instead, and his attention fixed on one rider in particular: a bowlegged man with a thin face and shaggy black hair who had forged out ahead of the others.

'That feller out front,' he gasped, pointing. 'I figure he must read sign. That's why we can't shake 'em off.'

Lee nodded. 'You know, now that I think on it, I know that *hombre* — seen him before, that time I helped drive them beeves down to Don Miguel's ranch, an' then again back in Concepción. He's some kinda half-blood, name'a . . . ' — he thought for a moment, then said, — 'Fausto Talon. A mighty unsociable cuss, as I recall.'

'Well, he's sure not doing *us* any favours,' said Will, starting back down to the horses, the shirt beneath his coveralls plastered to him with sweat, the rest of him powdered with dust.

'Come on. The border can't be too far now.'

What worried him, though, was the very real possibility that Don Miguel would follow them clear *across* the border, to avenge his son.

'You know somethin', Will?' Lee offered thoughtfully. It had been *Will*, as opposed to *sodbuster*, ever since they'd quit Concepción. 'I reckon we could shake those bastards for good, iffen someone was to take a shot at Talon.'

'*Me*, you mean.'

Lee shrugged, his right arm still hanging in the sling around his neck, the once-white bandage now frayed and stained. 'You're the gun-wizard.'

They'd spoken a little about the startling display Will had put on back in Concepción. Well, *Lee* had. Will hadn't said much about it, except to confirm that he'd learned to shoot during the war, and spent much of his time picking off Yankee officers as a Confederate sharpshooter.

Will considered the suggestion briefly, then remounted, gathered his reins and said, 'Come on, let's keep on the move.'

That same night, however, as Don Miguel's men — now reduced to a total of seven — sat around a small fire and ate a meagre supper of salt pork and beans, a shot boomed out of the darkness and Felix Talon reared up, screamed, twisted and fell to earth. A second shot followed hard on the first, and then one more, these bullets ploughing into the fire and sending embers spinning in all directions. Don Miguel threw himself backwards into cover and the rest of his men did likewise, and for a while there was a lot of shouting and wild return fire until the Don bellowed for silence.

In that silence they heard the fading sounds of a horse galloping north.

Coming out of his crouch, Don Miguel walked slowly back to the remains of the fire. One of his men, Joachin Ressal, called for him to be careful, but his only response was a bitter smile. 'He will not be back,' he called confidently and, as his shrewd brown eyes dropped to Fausto Talon, he muttered, 'He has done what he came to do.'

Slowly the rest of the Mexicans came out of cover and stared spookily into the night. One of them knelt beside Talon, who was rocking from side to side, his thin face screwed up in pain.

'How is he?' asked the Don, sliding his .38 back into its holster.

'He has been shot in the shoulder, *jefe*,' reported the *vaquero*.

Don Miguel nodded, unsurprised. *Si*, the shoulder. Another wound calculated to incapacitate but not kill. And another chance the *gringo* marksman had had to kill the Don himself, to have killed any *number* of them, which he had not taken.

He peered thoughtfully into the darkness. The *gringo* had shot Fausto in the forlorn hope that without him, the Don and his men would be unable to trail them. But they'd left it too late for that. This close to the border, there was only one route the *gringos* could take to reach the Rio Bravo now. All Don Miguel had to do was follow the same route himself.

He said, 'Maximo! You have some skill with wounds. Do what you can for Fausto now, and take him back to Concepción in the morning. The rest of you, saddle up.'

'Now, *jefe*?' asked Joachin Ressal doubtfully.

Don Miguel turned to face him. 'We ride through the entire night if we have to,' he grated. 'But by sunrise tomorrow, the buzzards will feast on the flesh of my son's killers: I swear it!'

★ ★ ★

Next morning, well before the sun had started its eastward climb, Will and Lee were back in the saddle.

Hunched against the cold grey dawn, they pushed down into a grassy saucer

201

of land at a steady, northward lope. The morning was quiet, the countryside around them, and the purple hills banking away to their left, empty and lifeless. As they rode, Lee continually flexed the fingers of his right hand.

'You all right?' asked Will.

'Damned arm feels stiff as a board.'

'Want me to take a look at it?'

'Naw. I'll get the army sawbones to check it over when we reach Camp Lincoln.'

Will smiled tiredly. 'Sometime later today, you reckon?'

'I'd lay money on it. That damn' border's so close now I can almost *smell* it.'

They rode on in silence for a while, until Will said, 'You figure on, ah, staying around town when we get back, Lee?'

'Not hardly. You remember what Mr Baylock said that day I saved your worthless hide? He told me to clear the county, an' that's jus' what I aim to do.'

'Well, don't be in too much of a

hurry to move on. I'd appreciate to introduce you to my wife first.'

Lee looked a little embarrassed. 'Aw, there ain't no need fer — '

'The hell there's not,' Will cut in firmly. 'I've never known another man I'd call a friend, Lee, but I reckon you've been the best friend I could've had through all this.'

Lee looked him in the face, very seriously, then swallowed and quickly faced front again. 'Well,' he said, his tone over-light, 'I guess we *have* knowed some times together this last couple'a weeks, ain't we?'

Even as Will opened his mouth to agree, a gunshot boomed out of nowhere, and the horses beneath them broke stride and turned skittish. Reaching for his Colt, Will threw a hasty glance behind him, saw half-a-dozen sombrero-topped horsemen spilling down into the valley he and Lee had just been crossing so leisurely and thought: *Don Miguel*!

In the handful of seconds that

followed he ran a gamut of emotions: shock, disappointment, fear and anger. Then, jabbing his heels into the paint pony's flanks, he bawled, 'Move it, Lee! Move it!'

As more shots peppered the pale dawnlight, the horses stretched out into a gallop. Will stabbed the Colt behind him, thumbed back, fired, thumbed back and fired again, his intention, as always, being to discourage, not kill.

But it wasn't going to work this time. Don Miguel wanted to finish it: his men wanted to finish it; and in their hurry to finish it they were willing to take chances — *any* chances.

The ground beneath the horses' driving hooves started to rise again, and the horses — like their riders, worn down by days of hard travelling and poor rations — dug in and thrust and laboured like hell to achieve the rolling ridge above. Up, up, higher, with Will and Lee leaning forward over tangled manes and pistol shots chasing them every step of the way.

And then they were there.

For just a moment, as the tired horses slowed, they were skylined against the lightening sky: then they dropped down towards the pale-grey mouth of a wide, twisting canyon a couple of hundred yards below, kicking up great billowing clouds of dust in their wake.

A bunch of seconds ticked into history, barely a minute's worth: then Don Miguel topped out and came blurring after them, standing in the stirrups and whipping his palomilla mercilessly with his split-ended reins, and right behind him came the remainder of his men, loosing off shots whenever they felt they stood a chance of hitting their quarry.

Will and Lee surged into the canyon at a reckless pace. Almost immediately the rocky defile narrowed and swung to the left. The paint pony, a ribby animal to start with, and one never meant for this kind of treatment, lost its footing, slipped in an explosion of dust and loose scree, then regained its balance and blurred on with Will, still an inexpert horseman, hanging on for dear life.

On, on, on . . .

Now there was nothing else in the whole wide world except this deep canyon with its boulder-strewn, rock-littered, snake-twisting floor and weathered walls. And *noise*: the roar of gunfire, the whine of lead, the *spang* of bullets powdering rock and then spinning off at crazy angles, and the thunderous clatter of horse-hooves as they drummed on through the ever-twisting defile.

And then, suddenly, the canyon fell behind them and the scrub- and brush-choked land sloped up toward the blue-white sky. Will drew level with Lee, and the first thing they saw when they topped out was a great, grassy plain rising gently to the west in a rock-strewn hill, and there, barely a mile directly ahead of them, a thin silver line reflecting the rising sun.

The Rio Grande.

The *border*!

Lee screamed, '*Whoo-eee!*' and Will very nearly joined him, but then they both caught a hint of movement away to the east, and above the rhythmic *thrub* of the straining horses, Will heard Lee curse.

A bad feeling made his guts clench as he fixed his eyes on the newcomers, a strung-out line of horsemen powering towards them at a hard run. They were Mexicans, he saw, gun-hung and dressed in drab olive-green uniforms.

'*Who are they?*' he yelled.

Lee bawled, '*Rurales!*'

'*Who* — ?'

'*The Mexican police, dammit!*' yelled Lee — and as the *rurales* started shooting at them, he swore again.

★ ★ ★

Dr Victor Gaines, Camp Lincoln's laconic, rail-thin army surgeon, was leaning against an examination table in his small office at the back of the post's

207

infirmary, enthusiastically discussing a requisition for medical supplies with his commanding officer, Major Chalmers, when the door suddenly burst open and Tom Peckover rushed in.

'You know, I just don't believe it,' he started: then, seeing Major Chalmers sitting in Gaines's visitor's chair, he drew up short, squared his shoulders and saluted smartly. 'Uh, begging the major's pardon.'

A tall, barrel-chested man with crinkly green eyes and mutton-chop side-whiskers the colour of dirty snow, Chalmers returned the salute and said, 'At ease, Tom. What is it you can't believe — unless, of course, it's a private matter between you and Dr Gaines?'

'Not at all, sir,' Peckover replied breathlessly. 'Actually, it's about Will Hooper.'

'The farmer whose wife was assaulted by that Mexican cattleman?'

'Yes, sir.'

'All right, Tom, spit it out.'

Peckover shrugged. 'Well, as you know, sir, I had a great deal of sympathy for the fellow, and not for one moment did I believe that report in yesterday's *Monitor*, about him murdering the Mexican. He was set on *arresting* the man, sir, not *killing* him.'

'And?' prodded Chalmers.

'Well, I've just come through town, and . . . and it seems that a number of the civilians there share my opinion. In fact, they feel so strongly about it that several of them are planning to ride south to help him!'

Speaking for the first time, Dr Gaines said, '*What*?'

Peckover shook his head dazedly. 'Don't ask me what's made them have a change of heart,' he said. 'But all of a sudden Hooper has more friends in Camp Lincoln than I would have believed possible.'

'That *is* amazing,' said Gaines.

Stroking his side-whiskers pensively, Major Chalmers said, 'The Mexicans plan to hang this fellow Hooper, don't they?'

'Reading between the lines, I believe that is the intention of the father of the boy they say he killed, yes, sir. But they'll have a fight on their hands if the men I saw just now reach him first, I can promise you.'

The major nodded. 'I do believe you're right,' he agreed. 'You know, Tom, I think it's time you took some leave.'

Peckover frowned at him. 'Beg pardon, sir?'

'You're on leave, Tom,' the major said more deliberately. 'Effective immediately.'

Peckover shook his head. 'I'm sorry, sir, I just don't — '

Gaines made a sound of impatience in his throat. 'Oh, for heaven's sake, Tom, get on over to your quarters, get out of that uniform and get yourself back into town. If those civilians plan to ride south as you claim, they'll need a good man to lead them, won't they?'

Understanding finally dawned, and Peckover threw up another salute. 'Oh, yes! I mean, right! I mean, I'm on my way!'

★ ★ ★

Twenty minutes later, dressed in a plaid shirt and grey canvas pants, Peckover hauled rein beside a dozen- or fifteen-strong group of mounted civilians who had congregated outside the sheriff's office. Sheriff Doyle was standing on the boardwalk in front of them, fists on hips.

'You men're crazy!' he was saying gruffly, as Peckover dismounted. 'You can't just go and take the law into your own hands, dammit! You there, Pardee! This time yesterday you were afraid there might be war with Mexico. Now you're just apt to start it yourself!'

'You finished yet, Sheriff?' asked one of the townsmen.

'No, I'm not!' barked Doyle, but without noticeable conviction. 'I'm

211

asking you all to reconsider! You go blundering across the border on your fool's errand and tangle with them Mexicans, it could come to shooting. Any of you stopped to think about that? That some of you might not come back?'

Another townsman, spotting Peckover as he climbed onto the boardwalk, said, 'Hey, look, the army's here!'

'What do you think, Cap'n?' asked Pardee. 'We're fixin' to ride south an' help that there farmer!'

Running his eyes over them all, Peckover said mildly, 'You men've changed your tune, haven't you? Wasn't so long ago you wouldn't give him the time of day.'

'Who cares that he's a sodbuster any more?' called a gravelly voice on the far side of the crowd. 'He's an *American*, ain't he? That's what counts. An' whether Hooper had any choice in killin' the Benedictus boy or not, I reckon he had it comin', what he did to Hooper's wife.'

Peckover arched one eyebrow in surprise. 'Well said, Mr Baylock.'

'You reckon we' doin' right, then?' asked the first townsman. 'Ridin' south to help that feller?'

'Not only that,' replied Peckover, 'I've come to join you.'

A cheer went up among some of the more enthusiastic civilians. 'Then what we waitin' for?' cried Lyle Payne, the bartender. 'Let's ride!'

As Peckover turned and went back to his horse, Ned Baylock heeled his charcoal stallion closer to Sheriff Doyle. 'Know you mean well, Frank,' he said in a confidential growl. 'But these men've made up their minds to save Hooper from the Mexicans, an' they're dead-set on goin' through with it.'

'Yeah — after *you* got 'em all fired up to do it,' Doyle replied sourly.

Baylock shrugged. 'Sometimes a man needs to have some sense talked into him.'

'I know that,' Doyle replied. 'And because I'm the sheriff around here, it's my job to caution you hot-heads against taking the law into your own hands. But if you really want to know why I'm so damned mad, it's not because I lost the argument.' And here he grinned suddenly. 'It's because I can't go with you, Ned.'

To his left, Peckover called, 'Ready, men?'

Baylock called back, 'I was *born* ready, Soldierboy!'

'Then let's make dust!' cried Peckover.

They did.

★ ★ ★

With the *rurales* riding east-to-west on a line that would cut them off long before they could reach the Rio Grande, and Don Miguel's riders closing on them from the south with every passing second, there was nothing else for it but to stand and fight.

Spotting a jumble of boulders midway up the hill to their left, Will shouted, 'Head for the rocks, Lee! We'll hold them off from there!'

But even as they turned their lathered animals and started up the slope, a bullet punched into Lee's buckskin, midway between hip and croup, and the horse lurched, screamed and went down heavily in a tangle of snapping legs.

Will screamed, 'Lee!'

But Lee was already reacting. Kicking free of the stirrups, he threw himself out of the saddle even as the buckskin went down, and hit the ground in a wild kind of stagger-run. Momentum pushed him on for another few yards until he was finally able to pull up, turn and run back to the dead horse, where he tore his Winchester from its scabbard. Only then did he start running again, this time for the safety of the rocks.

Knowing he must buy time for his companion to reach cover, Will drew rein, turned his mount back towards the nearest of their pursuers — the *rurales* — and emptied his Colt at them. They fanned out and slowed down a bit, but still kept coming, and he had no alternative but to turn the paint pony again and send it charging up the slope.

He and Lee made it to the rocks together, and as Will threw himself out of the saddle, Lee thrust the Winchester at him, and Will pitched him the empty Colt, snapping, 'Reload it!'

While Lee rummaged in Will's saddle-bags for cartridges, Will came up over the nearest rock, snap-aimed at the oncoming *rurales* and sent three fast shots into the ground directly in front of the lead rider, a jowly-faced lieutenant with a heavy black moustache. The lieutenant's mount reared up and pawed at the air, and the other *rurales* bunched up behind him, then spread out and galloped north, for the cover of a scattering of boulders and brush at the foot of the slope.

A couple of minutes later, Don Miguel's party arrived, blasting at the rocks as they rode fast by Will and Lee's position and reined in where the *rurales* had taken cover. There'd be some brief introductions down there now, Will thought grimly, a council of war, and then the shooting would start up all over again.

He glanced around, evaluating their situation. They occupied high ground, which gave them an advantage over their opponents, but they couldn't hold out indefinitely: sooner or later they'd run out of water, supplies and ammunition, and then they'd be Don Miguel's for the taking.

It didn't look good.

'They'll flank us, you know,' murmured Lee, breaking his train of thought. 'First chance they get, they'll send men to north an' south, to get around behind us.'

Will nodded. 'Then we'll give as good as we get,' he replied grimly, and offered his left hand.

Lee hesitated just a moment, then: 'You' damn' right we will,' he said, and they shook on it.

What the Mexicans tried to do first, though, was rush them.

Without warning, a heavy fusillade suddenly erupted from the brush and rocks down below, and the minute Will and Lee ducked, the *rurale* lieutenant and six of his men came charging up the hill on foot, blasting away with their bolt-action Mauser rifles.

Meeting the challenge, Will immediately came up over the rocks and started shooting back, and the lieutenant took a bullet in the leg, collapsed and rolled back down the hill, moaning. Holding his .44 left-handed, Lee shot another *rurale*, who fell and didn't move again. Three men threw themselves into cover nearby, the last one turned tail and ran.

The *rurales* who'd made it to cover halfway up the slope kept pouring lead at their position: rock splinters spun and flipped through the early morning air. One cut Will across the cheek and he flinched backwards, and at about the same time rock-dust sprayed Lee in the eyes, momentarily blinding him.

Taking advantage of the brief lull in return fire, a small, mixed force of *rurales* and *vaqueros* broke cover and sent their horses charging up the hill. Hearing them approach, Will came around the rocks, not over them, snap-aimed and fired the Winchester four times. One of the *rurales* cried out, stood up in the stirrups, hugged himself and then pitched backwards off his horse. The horse right beside him went down with a bullet in the chest, and its rider, Joachin Ressal, flew over its head, landed hard and rolled weakly.

Bellowing profanity, Lee emptied his .44 into their attackers, and when that ran dry he cast it aside and started using Will's now-reloaded Colt. Another *rurale* left his saddle and started limping back down to the cover of the rocks and brush below, holding himself tight.

But still they came, and it was nothing fancy, just a straight, frontal assault that Will and Lee couldn't hope to repel. Another of Don Miguel's *vaqueros* spilled sideways from his saddle, but then the rest of the Mexicans were there, crowding their little jumble of rocks, crowding *them* to make further gunplay impossible, and as much as he hated to admit it, Will knew that it was over: their desperate run for the border, whatever stand they'd been hoping to make here . . . all over.

One of the *rurales* spurred his horse at Lee, shoved him roughly aside, and as he fell he jarred his bandaged arm and cried out at the sudden, jabbing pain of it. Will made to go to him, took maybe three paces, and then another *rurale* rode up behind him and used the butt of his Mauser to club him to his knees.

Men dismounted, swore at them in Spanish, kicked them, tore their weapons away from them and then dragged them back to their feet and shoved them roughly down the slope, past the wounded and on towards Don Miguel, who watched them come.

At the foot of the slope one of the *rurales* snapped, '*Alto*!' and they slowed to a halt before the Don, who looked them up and down disdainfully, paying particular attention to Will, this man who had killed his son and could so easily have killed him at least twice.

'So,' he said after a while in soft, very good English. 'It ends.'

Will only returned his appraisal.

'Do you have anything to say before I take you and hang you?' asked the Don.

Head throbbing, Will sleeved blood away from his cut cheek. 'Would it do us any good?' he croaked.

'No.'

'I didn't think so. But for what it's worth, it was me fired the bullet that killed your boy. I didn't mean to kill him, though God knows he had it coming. I came here because I knew I'd never get him to stand trial for what he did to my wife unless I could get him back on American soil. That was the plan. But the fool went for his gun and gave me no choice but to shoot him before he could shoot *me*.'

'Expect neither sympathy nor mercy, señor,' said the Don grimly.

'I don't,' returned Will. 'But if I hang, I expect to hang for a better reason than ridding the world of your crazy son.'

Temper flaring, Don Miguel lashed out and slapped him across the face, and Will rocked back on his heels, then threw himself at Don Miguel.

What happened then happened quickly: he grabbed the Don and spun him roughly, thrust one arm around his throat and tore the .38 from his free hand.

'*No disparar!*' croaked the *rurale* lieutenant, trying to rise up from where he'd been resting his bloodstained leg, and waving his arms frantically at his men and the men who had been riding with the Don. 'Don't shoot!'

Will jammed the barrel of the .38 under Don Miguel's chin and said,

'That's it . . . no one move. Lee, tell one of these Mexicans to cut out three fast horses. Tell 'em you, me and Don Miguel are riding for the Rio together, and they better not try to stop us, 'cause I'll blow the Don's brains out if they do.'

Cracking a nervous grin, Lee nodded, turned and tore a pistol from the belt of the nearest *rurale*. Before he could translate Will's instructions, however, Don Miguel moved his head a little sideways, so that he could see his captor from the edge of his vision, and said in a thick, choked, confident voice, 'You're bluffing, *señor*. You won't hurt me. You *know* you won't.'

'Don't put money on that.'

'You could have killed me twice over since this chase began, but you didn't. Why was that?'

Before Will could reply, one of the Don's men suddenly turned his head and, stabbing a finger away to the north, yelled, '*Riders*!'

Almost immediately a band of

bunched-tight horsemen came rumbling into sight from the north, and Will knew a moment of unreality as he saw that they were Americans: more, that Ned Baylock was riding at their head, and so was Tom Peckover, though the captain was now dressed like a civilian.

Lee whispered, 'What in the *hell* . . . ?'

As he took in the scene which confronted them, Peckover raised one hand to slow and then halt the Camp Lincolners while they were still about fifty yards away. The captain showed little surprise at the tableau: it had, after all, been the sound of gunfire that had led them to this spot in the first place. But a bad situation could suddenly turn into a veritable bloodbath if it wasn't handled carefully.

He and Baylock came forward alone, at a more cautious pace, Peckover holding up one hand, palm out, to show that their intentions were peaceful.

Will heard Don Miguel say softly, 'Señor Ned?'

The air was charged with tension as the two Americans rode closer and then hauled in. Peckover called deliberately, 'It's all right now, Mr Hooper. There's no need for further bloodshed. Whatever's been happening here, it's . . . it's finished now, and we've come to give you safe passage out of Mexico.'

Will snorted, suddenly feeling dangerously light-headed. 'That true, Baylock?' he asked sceptically. 'Or is it more likely that you've come to help Don Miguel tie the noose, or dance on my grave?'

Ignoring that, Baylock dismounted, drew his cane from a saddle-sheath and shuffle-thumped closer. 'I'm askin' you to throw that gun away, Hooper,' he said in that low, gravelly rasp of his. 'It's like that soldier-boy jus' said: it's finished.'

'The hell you say!' said Lee, tightening his grip on the pistol.

Baylock stopped in front of the Don, looked him in the face and shook his head sadly, and Will was surprised to see genuine compassion in his piggy little eyes. 'How long we been friends, Miguel?' he asked almost gently. 'More years than either of us care to recall, ayuh? Well, you know me, I never could stand men like this here Hooper: sodbusters. But I'm takin' Hooper's side in this. You hear me? Alesandro did wrong, an' Hooper here had every right to come after him. You'd see that too, you could see what he did to Hooper's wife.'

Don Miguel looked him in the face and wanted to argue the point, but all he could hear in his mind was Rafael, what Rafael had said that night in Concepción. *There was a sickness in Alesandro. But we do not always care to acknowledge that which is distasteful to us, so we look the other way and pretend that things, and people, are not really the way they are.* And Felix Paesar: *Whatever they did, you can be sure your son deserved it.*

'He murdered my son,' he whispered helplessly.

'What happened to Alesandro was an accident,' Will said softly. 'What happened to my wife wasn't.'

And then, all at once, Don Miguel's shoulders dropped and he looked older than his years and dreadfully, dreadfully tired. Baylock said again, 'Reckon you can throw that gun aside now, Hooper.'

Will released his grip on Don Miguel, spun the .38 by the trigger-guard and handed the weapon back to him butt-forward.

With a distracted nod, the Don took the gun and shoved it away. 'Go,' he said after a long pause. 'Go in . . . peace.' And turning to face his men and the *rurales*, he called, 'Do you hear me? Our business here is finished, and . . . and these men are free to go!'

★   ★   ★

As the Don, his men and the *rurales* gathered up their wounded and rode south, Will said, 'I never thought I'd say

227

this, Baylock — but I'm beholden to you.'

Baylock shrugged. 'Bein' neighbourly is all,' he growled embarrassedly. 'But still an' all, I'd say this business's taught us all a thing or two. Like mebbe how we should learn to get along, you an' me.'

'That's all I've ever wanted,' said Will.

'Then let's see what we can do about it, ayuh?' rasped Baylock, and he shoved out his hand.

Will shook with him, shook with Peckover too, when the young officer came over.

'How's my wife?' he asked urgently.

'Sick to death of the Camp Lincoln infirmary,' Peckover replied with a smile. 'At her insistence, I took her home yesterday morning. I imagine she's there, waiting for you, right now.'

'Then I'll make sure I don't keep her waiting any longer than I have to,' said Will.

He turned to Lee, and they studied

each other seriously for a moment, until Will said, thickly, 'Thanks, Lee. For everything.'

Lee shrugged. 'T'weren't nothin', not really.'

'The hell with that. You go get your arm checked over, and then you get yourself out to my place first thing tomorrow. You got some healing to do, and I'd be obliged if you'd do it out on the farm.'

Lee snorted. 'You reckon a stove-in cowpoke like me could stand livin' like a sodbuster?'

'There's only one way to find out.'

Lee's eyes shone briefly. 'I'll be there,' he said.

★ ★ ★

Don Miguel's party had travelled barely half a mile when one of his *vaqueros* suddenly called, '*Jefe*!'

Coming out of his reverie, the Don glanced around at the man, then turned to look in the direction he was indicating so urgently.

A lone horseman was skylined on a jagged ridge about a quarter-mile away, watching them.

Recognizing him, Don Miguel said, 'Wait here,' then heeled his palomilla across the intervening grassland and up the rolling slope towards the watcher. As soon as he reined down, Rafael Ugarte said apologetically, '*Perdon, jefe*. I know you told me to leave Coahuila, but I . . . I had to see for myself how your quest turned out first.'

Don Miguel studied the big man carefully. 'And you *did* see?' he said.

'*Si, jefe.*'

'And did you approve?'

'I am but a lowly servant, *jefe*. It is not for me to pass such a judgement. In any case, it is more important that *you* approve.'

'I will,' whispered the Don. 'In time.'

He suddenly gave a strange, self-conscious, choking kind of laugh. 'Ah, it is good to see you again, wise one,' he said sincerely. 'I was wrong to banish you, Rafael, and wrong not to have listened to you sooner. These past few days have been a trial. I still ache with loss. But . . . but it does my heart good to see you again.'

'If you will take me back,' said Rafael, 'I would be proud to serve you, *jefe.*'

Don Miguel swallowed. 'Come, then,' he said. 'Let there be no more talk of blood, and death, and sorrow. Let us go home side by side, as *compañeros* and remember the good times, *si*?'

'*Si, jefe,*' said Rafael, as he urged his horse forward and fell into step beside his master.

THE END

We do hope that you have enjoyed reading this large print book.

Did you know that all of our titles are available for purchase?

We publish a wide range of high quality large print books including:
Romances, Mysteries, Classics
General Fiction
Non Fiction and Westerns

Special interest titles available in large print are:
The Little Oxford Dictionary
Music Book, Song Book
Hymn Book, Service Book

Also available from us courtesy of Oxford University Press:
Young Readers' Dictionary
(large print edition)
Young Readers' Thesaurus
(large print edition)

For further information or a free brochure, please contact us at:
Ulverscroft Large Print Books Ltd.,
The Green, Bradgate Road, Anstey,
Leicester, LE7 7FU, England.
Tel: (00 44) **0116 236 4325**
Fax: (00 44) **0116 234 0205**